SHREWD LITTLE SLEUTH

Published October 2025
by Indies United Publishing House, LLC

Edited by Jen Z. Marshall

Cover Art by Craig Brown

FIRST EDITION

ISBN: 978-1-64456-853-8 [Hardcover]
ISBN: 978-1-64456-854-5 [Paperback]
ISBN: 978-1-64456-855-2 [Kindle]
ISBN: 978-1-64456-856-9 [ePub]
ISBN: 978-1-64456-857-6 [Audiobook]

Library of Congress Control Number: 2025917758

INDIES UNITED PUBLISHING HOUSE, LLC
P.O. BOX 3071
QUINCY, IL 62305-3071
INDIESUNITED.NET

ALSO BY SCOTT LECKIE

World Citizenship: Origins, Obstacles, Prospects (2025)

Mr. Housing Rights: The Joyous Highs and Devastating Lows of an Eccentric Human Rights Life (Forthcoming, 2025)

Exploring the Rights of Climate Displaced Persons (2025)
(with Shaun Butta)

One Earth, One Politics: Our Shared Path Toward World Citizenship (2025)
(with Pablo Rueda)

Before a Democracy Died: Housing, Land, and Property Rights in Myanmar (2024)
(with José Maria Arraiza)

Housing, Land, and Property Rights: Residential Justice, Conflict Zones, and Climate Change (2023)

The UN Principles on Housing and Property Restitution for Refugees and Displaced Persons, the Pinheiro Principles: A Commentary (2016)
(with Khaled Hassine)

Repairing Domestic Climate Displacement: The Peninsula Principles (2015)
(editor with Chris Huggins)

Land Solutions to Climate Displacement
(ed, 2014)

The Climate Change and Displacement Reader (2012)
(edited with Ezekiel Simperingham and Jordan Bakker)

Conflict and Housing, Land, and Property Rights: A Handbook on Issues, Frameworks, and Solutions (2011)
(with Chris Huggins)

Housing, Land, and Property Rights in Burma: The Current Legal Framework (2010)
(with Ezekiel Simperingham)

Housing, Land, and Property Rights in Post-Conflict UN and Other Peace Operations: A Comparative Survey and Proposal for Reform *(2009)*

Housing, Land, and Property Restitution Rights of Refugees and Displaced Persons: Laws, Cases, and Materials *(2007)*

Economic, Social, and Cultural Rights: Cases and Materials *(2006)*
(with Anne Gallagher)

Returning Home: Housing and Property Restitution Rights of Refugees and Internally Displaced Persons (2003)
(editor)

National Perspectives on Housing Rights *(2003)*
(editor)

When Push Comes to Shove (1995)

Destruction by Design (1994)

From Housing Needs to Housing Rights (1992)

www.scottleckie.com.au

Table of Contents

He was a G-Man. He was a lady's man. And given with whom he worked and where he hung out, he was probably a man's man too. He was a big drinker.

And a super spy.

Two decades after his excruciating dismissal from the FBI he loved so much, he married J. Edgar Hoover's secretary. Did he love her?

He worked with Marilyn Monroe, Joseph McCarthy, Howard Hughes, Marlon Brando, and many more.

A FOIA search unearthed 533 documents from the FBI, but they withheld ninety more. What didn't they want the world to know?

He was the father of my father, who never spoke about him. He was also the man whose legacy I inherited, and because of that, more than a little familial karmic cleansing has been required.

This is the story of my grandfather, Arthur Bernard Leckie, a shrewd little sleuth who might have known just enough to get him killed thirty-six hours before Marilyn's death just up the road.

Shrewd Little Sheuth

Scott Leckie

INDIES UNITED
PUBLISHING HOUSE, LLC

Introduction

Bringing My Father's Father Back to Life

Sometimes, a single person can encapsulate an entire era. A single lifetime can entwine the strands of history, providing a reasonably clear vision of life so many decades ago. And when that person to whom that lifetime belonged was a grandfather you never knew, there's invariably a story to be discovered and told.

As a child, my grandfather, Arthur Bernard Leckie (ABL), remained a mystery to me. I recently discovered part of the extraordinary life he had led—this jolly, heavy-drinking, Hollywood Noir incarnate straight out of a Raymond Chandler novel. More than once, the newspapers of the day praised him, though the term "a shrewd little sleuth" lacks the intended compliment.

My father never spoke of his father to anyone, but I inherited his legacy. This mysterious man is a part of me, and I will forever be a part of him. I, his progressive, international human rights lawyer grandson whom, of course, he never met, was more than a little puzzled by recent discoveries I made that my grandfather was deeply connected to the US empire and numerous client regimes.

As a globetrotting writer and human rights activist, I have spent my life working in over eighty countries with several of the NGOs, the

United Nations (UN), and organizations I founded. I've always fought for human rights for everyone, everywhere, and never given up on my vision of a unified humanity where all enjoy every human right, every moment of their lives. Indeed, it has gotten stronger as the years have rolled by, faster and faster with each passing year. I do not see people as their nationalities or citizenships. These are invisible to me, except when such identities are used as grounds for discrimination or oppression by another, more dominant, group; at that point, they become all-encompassing. Under normal circumstances, however, I see people as people; all of us are inherent parts of the human family —none more or less important than any other. A single species of *homo sapiens* all sharing a single planet.

Imagine my distress, therefore, when I first learned about my grandfather's work and how it seemed to run counter to all my life's efforts in a small way. It seems up to me to enact some form of familial karmic cleansing to undo the sins of my grandfather. How could I, a perpetual Green Party voter, writer and international human rights lawyer dedicated to alleviating the suffering of the poor, reconcile with a family background involving some of the worst human rights abuses witnessed in 20th-century US history?

Near the end of this process, I suddenly realized that today I am the sleuth; I am sleuthing the sleuth. Perhaps—if I am lucky—I may just out-sleuth the shrewd little sleuth and find out my grandfather's absolute identity. How did he view the world? How ambitious was he? Did he cut corners? Was all that schmoosing just a show? Was he power-hungry? Did he seek fame and fortune, or did his version of justice drive him more than anything else? How easily did he love— and whom did he love? What was it that drove him to drink? How close was he really to Hoover and all the other closeted men of power with whom he (perhaps quite literally) rubbed shoulders with during his career? Was ABL a heretofore secret kind of "friend" to Hoover, much like the more famous Melvin Purvis or Guy Hottel, whose lives became increasingly entwined with Hoover's as time rolled on? Was ABL kind and compassionate? Or was he cruel and selfish? Was he an assassin? Was he murdered?

Even more interesting to me is the quest to answer: How much would my granddad and I have had in common? What joys would we have shared, and where would we have diverged? How would each of us have considered decisions when confronted with challenging questions and choices that could determine our life pathways?

After more than sixty years, I have uncovered some mysteries surrounding the colorful and topsy-turvy life of my grandfather, ABL, who was involved in major American political events. Though I never met my paternal granddad, we share a lot: two of my three names, a quarter of my genetic make-up, and more than a few character traits that I have just now discovered. Some of these I happily embrace. Others, not so much.

I learned that less than thirty-six hours before dying in highly suspicious circumstances, surrounded by intrigue, mystery, and all the rest, he energetically danced for joy upon hearing the date of my impending birth, his first grandchild. Knowing now of his happiness about my pending arrival into this world instinctively brings me closer to this mysterious man. But as I've also discovered in this sixty-second year since his death, in our worldviews and the choices we made in our working and personal lives, we had more than a few deviations, some of which are as different as could be, with others nothing short of terrifying.

As a lifelong social justice fighter, it's more than a tad difficult to reconcile my embrace of humanity with the life of this quintessential American family member. He engaged in spying, secret investigations, planting bugs and wiretaps, and exposing people for their political views. He calculated proximity to some of the most foul and destructive American political figures of the past century.

Perhaps I intuitively knew there was a need to clear the somewhat fouled air when I chose a life dedicated to human rights, even though I knew so little about ABL when I embarked on my global life. But despite all this, he was my granddad, my dad's dad, and all these decades later, I want to know this peculiar man more now. I want to try to bring him back to life so I can more deeply understand both him and me better.

Thanks to this intriguing figure finding himself, or more likely placing himself, right at the center of a series of critical historical epochs and events from the 1930s until his unexpected death in California in the early 1960s, there is just enough information out there still to give me a strong sense of the very full life he lived. In the days immediately after his death, there was so much more, but thanks to my highly conscientious and legally fearful father, off went 99.9% of that into the paper shredder and fire, never to be seen again. Three hundred boxes of immaculately kept files are gone for good.

But in putting all of the remaining pieces of this story together for the first time, instead of soothing any curiosity I might have had about ABL, I feel a sense of disquiet about both the man himself and what he endured in both private and professional realms. The very real possibility that his death did not only occur out of the blue but was brought upon him by something seriously sinister haunts me to the core.

My granddad left this life just a few short months before I was born in the same town where he died, the City of Angels, Los Angeles. He passed away at the young and tender age of fifty-seven when my dad was just twenty-nine, the exact age I was when I started learning some of the details of the following, extraordinary story. Given the grief I felt at my dad's sudden demise when I was well into my fifties, I still wonder how my father, just short of three decades old, dealt with his dad's equally unexpected death under nothing less than bewildering circumstances.

Although perhaps reminiscent to some as a sort of Walter Mitty-like character who lived in a fantasy world of sought-after but elusive meaning, this intriguing man was, in fact, far more like a real-life Forrest Gump. He seemed to be strategically placed right in the middle of a series of major historical events during his adult life. Gump was there meeting President Kennedy, seeing action in the Viet Nam War, finding himself right in the center of the anti-war movement of the 1960s, and experiencing the early, tragic days of AIDS firsthand. ABL was a core part of the early days of the FBI, at Pearl Harbor during World War II, managing security at the founding meeting of the UN, working as a spy for the stars, heading investigations with the anti-communist and human rights violating McCarthy witch hunts, and so much more. And then, there are all those links to Marilyn Monroe during her (and his) final days ...

My dad never mentioned his father as I grew up in Southern California before I decided to very intentionally and permanently expatriate myself from the United States at the age of twenty-two. As a result, I spent my youth with almost no knowledge of the life of my grandfather other than a single memento, a hand-drawn penciled portrait—described by the artist Jerry Doyle as a cartoon—of ABL with a similar-looking man looming over him, as if intentionally placing himself into a position of suggestive domination, a hand sensually laid onto ABL's right shoulder. This unsettling drawing was presented to ABL at a testimonial dinner given in his honor on February 27, 1939, held at the Penn Athletic Club in Philadelphia, where he headed the local FBI office. A word bubble quote, which I memorized as a child, extends from the mouth of the speaker, says, "Leckie is one of our most outstanding agents. It is men like he that have made the organization what it is today." That agent was my granddad. The organization was the FBI. And the man to whom we can attribute that quote turned out to be none other than the controversial, first, and multi-decade boss of the Federal Bureau of Investigation (FBI), J. Edgar Hoover. A letter thanking Doyle and ABL for the cartoon from Hoover lets us know that he gratefully received a copy of this strange drawing of one of the FBI's first employees.

As a child, I was thankfully not brought up in a religious household, though parts of the Leckie clan were and still are deeply religious, fundamentally so. In one of the few attempts by my parents to interest me in the pursuit of eternal life, I was forced to attend a session of Sunday school at a local Presbyterian church. Though only eleven years old, I felt so averse to this idea that I intentionally shut the index finger of my left hand into the door of my maternal grandmother's yellow *Corvair*—a notoriously dangerous car model made famous by Ralph Nader's book *Unsafe at Any Speed*—breaking the finger in the process and wailing in so much agony that I permanently avoided joining the God Squad. And yet, despite my early aversion to deity-based beliefs, as much as I may respect people's wishes to have soul-soothing faith in such things, for a time during my early years, I was nonetheless somehow instilled with an overwhelming sense of fear of an all-powerful god. This god controlled everything, punishing those who strayed from righteousness. In my juvenile mind's eye, Hoover loomed over my seated and subservient grandfather, like God himself. Whenever I would think of God, it was not the image of an old White man with a beard floating in the sky but the wavy hair of Hoover, who amassed god-like powers that destroyed the lives of a great many people, my granddad included. Knowing what we know now, all these decades later, with his right hand visible atop ABL's shoulder, the absence of his left hand raises questions.

Known by many names, including The Bulldog and even The State Within the State, Hoover infamously ran the FBI with an iron grip for nearly fifty years, throughout the terms of eight successive presidents, starting with the driving force behind the League of Nations, Woodrow Wilson in 1924, and ending with the disgraced and corrupt Richard Nixon in 1972. Among other highly questionable practices, Hoover notoriously compiled and kept compromising career-destroying files on numerous major politicians or other people of influence in the country. Far from dedicating himself solely to the important work of protecting the American population from criminals and the crimes they committed, he instrumentally turned many elements of the leading domestic law enforcement agency in the US into tools of oppression and nothing less than human rights abuses.[1] Hoover demanded blind loyalty from his staff. He imparted an organizational worldview known by all who worked under him: if any information came to light involving the White House or high echelons of political power, it would be brought to his attention first, presumably to bolster the secret files. Hoover intentionally instilled fear in countless people, and his once sterling reputation during the first decades of the FBI spiraled markedly downwards toward the end

---

[1] There are numerous books written about Hoover's misdeeds, and among many others, any of Athan Theoharis' 23 books will reveal every single tidbit of the FBI leader's often unsavory ways of doing things. For those interested, consider starting your reading with this: Athan Theoharis, *Spying on Americans: Political Surveillance from Hoover to the Huston Plan,* Temple University Press, 1978.

of his life as his more dubious methods and agenda became more widely known.

One writer recounted the views of former Acting Attorney General Laurence Silberman, the first person to peruse Hoover's secret files after his death, who noted that, "J. Edgar Hoover was like a sewer that collected dirt. I now believe he was the worst public servant in our history."[2] The sheer scale of his secret files is staggering. Hoover kept hundreds of files in his office comprising 17,750 pages, many of which held compromising sexual material on at least 164 people.[3] Presidents, politicians, entrepreneurs, actors, activists, and others feared Hoover, but my acquiescent granddad did not—at least not initially.

Hoover was once untouchable but no longer. Now, more than fifty years after his death, growing voices request a renaming of the FBI headquarters building, which is named after Hoover, because of his controversial views and practices.[4] His legacy is rightfully tarnished forever; there is no doubting that.

In early August 1992, several years after my human rights life began[5], I briefly returned to Southern California with my Dutch girlfriend, whom I was living with in Utrecht at the time. One night, we took my dad out to dinner at a small Italian bistro on Balboa Island in Newport Beach, and much to my amazement, after a few glasses of excellent dry white wine, my dad—a rare teardrop forming in his eye —suddenly blurted out, "My dad died thirty years ago today." Because he *never* spoke about his dad during my early years, he stunned me by even mentioning him. My dad's cousin, Chuck Leckie, believes that it took my father thirty years to begin spilling the beans simply because, in a heartbreakingly truthful remark that I fear is all too accurate, my

---

[2]Anthony Summers, *The Secret Life of J. Edgar Hoover*, Pocket Books, 1993, p. 221.

[3]Curt Gentry, *J. Edgar Hoover: De Man en Zijn Geheimen* (English: J. Edgar Hoover: The Man and His Secrets), Toren Boeken, 1991, p. 29.

[4]https://www.latimes.com/opinion/story/2022-05-02/j-edgar-Hoover-name-fbi-director-fbi-building-racist-homophobic-legacy.

[5]My forthcoming memoir, *Mr. Housing Rights: The Joyous Highs and Devastating Low of an Eccentric Human Rights Life* gives detailed accounts of many elements of my ongoing human rights career. See also: www.scottleckie.com.au.

dad tragically "didn't want his dad to be a part of him." ABL—as we all have—had many sides, some good, some not so good, and some of these deeply affected my father long after his father's death. The elements of his personality and lifestyle that may have disturbed my sensitive dad are one thing. The central role he played in pivotal political moments, some of which became shameful events in US history, is something else entirely.

By this time, I had been politically active throughout the world for several years. I understood the importance of protecting human rights and, thus, just how dangerous a man Hoover turned out to be. I jumped at the chance of finally asking my dad to tell us something more than what that strange drawing depicted. In 1992, all I knew were a handful of FBI stories and the creepy cartoon; everything else I've learned started that night, increasing again in the past few months while I began writing this story. Somehow, this anniversary loosened something within my father, heavily helped, I suspect, by the effects of the wine on a man who never drank too much, starkly contrasting with his heavily alcoholic father. That evening, he let loose, unloading an incredible array of stories about the life of his father, none of which I had ever heard before.

My grandfather was born in Alabama, although I always thought he was born in New Jersey, the place ABL went to live briefly after his stint at the FBI ended. I knew of our family links to the American South, a place so different from the gentle coastal Southern California life of Orange County that I grew up in, but I never imagined that ABL grew up there. During my early years, I didn't really understand the implications of this, even though my first name was inherited from ABL's sister, my Great Aunt Mary Scott Godbold, whom people called Scottie.

Without knowing the area's history or the gruesome details of the US Civil War, the Confederacy, slavery, segregation, the Ku Klux Klan, George Wallace, and others, I loved visiting Mary Scott and her stern husband, John, when I was quite young. Everything felt different the second we disembarked at Montgomery Airport. It was like entering another world, something which surely must have helped to spark my lifelong love of travel and visiting new and unknown places.

It is difficult to describe the feeling of awe that occurs every time I visit a new place, something I have had the good fortune to feel hundreds upon hundreds of times over the years. We would drive what seemed a great distance from Mary Scott and John's house in the small town of Camden after drinking overly sweet homemade lemonade with still not-yet-dissolved sugar granules visible at the bottom of the condensation-laden glass—a desperate attempt to cool off from the oppressive humidity of the South. We would then reach a catfish restaurant located on a dark, gloomy, moss-covered bayou, where I was transported back in time to a place I could have never imagined existed in the real world.

Much of the information I've learned about my grandfather I gained through a successful FOIA search in 2002 that resulted in the acquisition of a tantalizingly thick box of over five hundred pages of FBI documents mentioning ABL and a vast array of his activities during his time at the Bureau from 1934–1939. Opening this box and leafing through these decades-old documents all about my granddad was a magical experience, like discovering buried treasure. The man I never knew suddenly came to life. In equal measure, however, it was also an immensely strange and somewhat disquieting feeling to hold copies of letters in my hands, the originals of which were once held by the hands of the infamous Hoover, with a still fresh-looking ink signature of the man who did so much to push American democracy and, in the end, my grandfather to the brink. One thing that stood out, though, was the indication in the cover letter from the Department of Justice that "623 pages(s) were reviewed, and 533 page(s) are being released." What might be hiding in those missing ninety pages? What could lurk there that the DOJ doesn't want to world to learn about?

From the late 1940s to the early 1960s, when he would visit his family, ABL, this new man, so positively impacted by the free-spirited energy of the West Coast, became a hero to many. His nephew Larry Godbold remembered that "As a kid, Uncle Bernard was like Superman. Having an uncle in the FBI and having all these stars as clients, my claim to fame was him. When he'd greet me, he'd reach into his pocket and pull out ten or more quarters, which seemed like a million dollars."

It was around this time that the issue of alcohol again came up. Larry told me, "Your grandfather was awfully colorful and had a great personality. He did like to drink a lot, which surprised me. We had a phone in the hall right outside my room, and sometimes, he would call real late at night to my mother (his sister), and I think he was calling from a bar. She was very supportive of him." I guess he used to like to drink and dial.

ABL, Bunny to his closest friends and family, was my father's father. He naturally died (or was killed), it's still not clear which, four months before I was born. He lived veiled in the world of the FBI's highest echelons and at the pinnacle of America's secrets and lies. But his true desires may have forced him to live a life cloaked in a closet because society didn't want to see what it preferred to ignore. It left the telling of his extraordinary life to a grandson he never knew.

In the pages that follow, I seek to bring out the man and his larger-than-life personality by recounting many of the major highs and lows of a truly interesting life. What follows is anything but a hagiography. It is entirely absent of any, at least intentional, palimpsest. More than anyone, I want to know the truth and what made my grandad tick. Whom did he love? What did he loathe? What did he do well? Where did he fail? Where did he go in his free time? What was his favorite drink? What did he believe in? How free or unfree did he feel? Did any swords of Damocles hang perpetually over his head? Did he live and die a happy and contented man, or did his demons come back to haunt him one by one?

In seeking answers to these and other queries, almost unintentionally, I came to know my grandad in previously unimagined ways. After six decades of him playing almost no role whatsoever in my life, I now know him so well that he frequently comes to me in my dreams, where we face each other smiling, conversing about a plethora of topics, our conversations always ending before he can answer the biggest question of all, "How did you *really* die, Grandad?"

Chapter I

From Mystery to Intrigue

Greenville, Alabama, in the early twentieth century, was as far from the birthplace of liberalism, understanding, and equality as one could get. People accepted discrimination as a fact of life. People knew their place. Religious rituals ruled the day. ABL, born in Greenville on February 5, 1905, grew up poor in the Deep South, in an American state considered by many to be well behind much of the rest of America politically, economically, and—particularly—socially. A recent voting rights case before the US Supreme Court attests to the sad fact that Alabama has very much yet to shake its obsession with race.

ABL was often absent from school for unexplained reasons, resulting in unimpressive grades, mainly Cs and Ds, except for his final year, when he mostly received As. During high school from 1919–1923, he worked at Peagler Drug Co. in the afternoons and evenings, and according to his boss, ABL was "always reasonable, persistent, though a bit slow to learn."

In the first of numerous alcohol references, an FBI pre-hire background investigation noted that although "he had known Bernard to drink a little but that otherwise he is of good moral character and would make a good man for anyone."

According to the same report, we find the following views from one of his high school principals: "Mr. A.A. Miller, Asst. Principal, Butler High School, stated that he knows Bernard very well and has played golf with him a lot. Miller advises… that he ran the mile on the track team. Miller further stated that Leckie was polished and very smooth, takes an occasional drink, but not in excess, and is from one of the best families in Greenville, his parents being very strict with their children, who have never been permitted to run around much…"

Over time, he became a football star and long-distance champion on the track. However, if a school essay from 1923 indicated his emerging political views before leaving the South, they significantly diverged from those of his grandson. He might have been as uncomfortable with people of other countries or colors as expected for someone from that insular, race-obsessed state, though his views later seem to have softened somewhat. This handwritten paper, worryingly entitled "The Immigration Problem" abhorred how the US—*the* archetypal immigrant country—was being swamped by immigrants and that constituted "one of the greatest social problems of America today," in a classic old-immigrant versus new-immigrant sentiment. Today, just over one hundred years later, these very same sentiments pervade US politics in a most repulsive manner, instilling fear in millions of people who blindly follow a strangely colored man and a political party increasingly standing for hatred, racism, selfishness, and nationalism. How little things seem to have changed.

ABL has been described by the very few living family members who knew him personally in various ways. Some painted him as very outgoing, very colorful, gregarious, and bubbly but also as a networker, very schmoozy, and even a bull shitter. Greenville's narrow-minded environment likely influenced his decision to leave the South for the seemingly limitless possibilities of California. The part of Alabama where ABL grew up didn't fare very well following the South's loss in the US Civil War, with the population in 1960 considerably smaller than in 1860. The local economy suffered following the war and The Reconstruction, leading to large-scale out-migration by those seeking greener pastures. And the pastures couldn't be greener than the glitz, glamour, and promise of Tinsel Town.

Within months of finishing high school, he was shipped off to the University of Southern California (USC) in Los Angeles, as far away from Greenville as possible. His all-expenses-paid education may have been the reparation ABL's parents had demanded to reclaim their son's soul and protect their name after rumors of impropriety had done the rounds in that tight-knit, deeply conservative, small town. It was probably not the best place for the imagined spiritual regrowth his parents envisioned, but Bunny liked it. There was booze, parties, and the beach—not exactly being exiled to purgatory.

In the mid–1920s, ABL found his way west, where he attended and graduated from USC with a degree in business administration in 1928. That same year, he married my grandmother, whom I knew well and spent much time with until she departed this Earth when I was ten. Lorene D. Leckie, an immensely sweet and kind woman, divorced ABL in 1958—another family secret—then moved to a little home in Corona Del Mar in Southern California. She lived out her days alone, often making her grandkids creamy and rich custard with nutmeg grated on top, served in little white ramekins. During my childhood I assumed my granddad had died young before I was born, unaware my grandparents had divorced. I'm not sure how I would have taken it had I known as a child that he didn't simply let my nana go but turned around and promptly married a woman who worked for years as Hoover's personal secretary!

Once he had left home for good, for many years, ABL would regularly drive a new Buick to Alabama to visit his parents, sometimes from LA and other times the more reasonable distance from DC, Charlotte, or Philadelphia, where he worked in various FBI offices. During one of those visits, his nephew recalled him getting out of the car at a gas station with Larry's father, John, at the wheel. John not only questioned ABL about getting out of the car but also wondered why he was speaking so jovially to the stranger who was filling the car with gasoline—the custom at the time. This outgoing, new Californian and once quiet Southerner replied, "I just wanted to talk to the guy, practice my craft, and get to know him," something that stood out in the rural South where class and racial distinctions were dominant features of the society, which remained unwilling to accept the results and consequences of the Civil War. This interaction took place during the 1950s, at a time when the KKK was very present and when schools in Little Rock, Arkansas, were famously just becoming integrated, with Black and White children finally able to attend the same schools.

ABL favored ending segregation, influenced by the more progressive ways of California and later the East Coast. He forcefully argued that it should happen in schools across America—not just in Little Rock. Larry recalled, "He'd been drinking a bit and got into a bit of an argument with my daddy, a friendly argument, but we didn't argue about anything, even a friendly argument, and they were talking about the integration of Little Rock. Daddy made a sweeping comment like, 'Oh, that's just an isolated event; they'll never integrate the whole of the US. If it takes thousands of soldiers to get one kid into school, they will never be able to do that in the whole US; there's not enough people to make integration work.'"

Unlike many White men in the deep South, ABL's brother-in-law John was not seen as outwardly racist. However, integration was not a popular subject in Alabama in the 1950s, leading his son, Larry, to reveal that amongst most White families in the area, integration was "not even on the table to discuss." As this discussion went on, spiraling dangerously into an argument about race, at one point, ABL interjected, "How can you talk like that? That's stupid."

Even if he didn't embrace it, ABL seemingly accepted the logic and reality of integration. All these years later, the economic, social, and political hardships, discrimination, and inequality facing Black Americans and other people of color in the US, especially in the South, remain staggering. White household median net worth in the US in 2025 shockingly remains ten times higher than Black American household median net worth. In virtually every other social and economic indicator, serious inequities remain. Although Black American players might now dominate Alabama's always powerful college football team, it took the performance of a single Black American player from their rival USC, Sam "The Bam" Cunningham, in a game between these teams in 1970, to begin what became a rather sudden end to Alabama's all-White team. (Incidentally, ABL, my dad, and my mother attended that university.) According to one commentator, former player Jerry Claiborne, this game did "more for integration in Alabama in sixty minutes than Martin Luther King Jr. did in twenty years." In 1971, Alabama's first African American football player, John Mitchell, made history and started for the Crimson Tide.[6]

Once ABL finished his studies at the university that would one day help to integrate Alabama's famous football team, things started to get interesting. He began his unsuspecting transformation into a kind of Mr. Everywhere, slotting himself into key events in US history but usually just one small step from the top. Soon after graduating from USC, he landed a job as an investigator for the Retail Credit Company in Los Angeles, where he worked from 1928–1934: a profession he continued to work in until the end of his life.

Many years later, sitting in an Italian restaurant on Balboa Island in Newport Beach, Southern California's high-density, warm weather answer to the informal luxury of the upper crust hideaways in Rhode Island's Newport, I sat across from ABL's only son, my father. He was in his fifties; I was not yet thirty. I wanted the stories I'd never heard. Also nicknamed Bunny, Attorney Bernard Leckie, also a graduate of USC, successfully represented sporting stars, ordinary citizens, as well as some of Hollywood's elite.

After someone opened the second bottle of Rombauer Chardonnay, I asked the question I'd waited to query: "What can you tell me about your father?"

"Listen, tiger," we all have our animals to bare, "let's not spoil a lovely meal ..."

I let out a long, disappointed sigh. He looked at me and then took a sip of the fruity and fresh chardonnay. As he set the glass down, he looked at his hands for a moment, and then, with resignation, as if he were about to explain the birds and the bees, he said, "Fine."

"I suspect you're talking about his time with the FBI and J. Edgar Hoover."

---

[6] https://www.theatlantic.com/entertainment/archive/2013/11/the-integration-of-college-football-didnt-happen-in-one-game/281557/.

"Yeah, but I want to hear all of it: J. Edgar, the UN, McCarthy, Howard Hughes, Marilyn ..."

My father took another, and longer, sip of wine. "I don't know all that much."

That wasn't true. He had destroyed almost all of those boxes of my grandfather's papers and files for some reason so many decades ago.

"What about all his files you shredded and burned?"

"Those shouldn't have been seen by anyone, ever. They were way too dangerous to keep around."

My father truly destroyed hundreds of my grandfather's archived files. When I finally got to what was left, there was just a fraction of what there would have been, had my father not been so conscientious. What I knew was that my grandfather was a hard-drinking man who had forged a life that my father was ambiguously both embarrassed by and secretly driven by. Little did I know at the time, but I, too, would spend much of my adult life trying to repay the world for the transgressions of my gregarious progenitor.

It turned out we were both trying to do the same thing: make the world a better place. We just went about it in very different ways.

ABL's first residence in Southern California was a home located at 737 N. Kinmore Ave, where he lived from May to November 1924. Then, he moved to 335 W. 27th Street. The latter home no longer exists, having been demolished and replaced with large government buildings bordering on one of LA's famous freeways. During those first weeks and months, in an environment as different as possible from the rural dirt roads of racially charged Alabama, he wrote frequently to his mother, often daily, a practice he continued throughout much of his life. Many of these were simply short postcards with pictures indicative of their era. The cards span decades —the 1920s, 30s, 40s, and 50s—and holistically reading them reveals succinct periods of his life.

The first batch come from a cross-country road trip by car in the mid-1920s, on his way across the country to his new home on the West Coast, a trip that must have been a rarity during those years. In a way, it reminds me of my early heroes Kerouac and Cassidy—Dean

Moriarty and Sal Paradise—in their *On The Road* travails, which took place just three decades later. ABL seems to have sent cards every morning from every place where he and two male friends, Frank Crosby and Bob Greene, spent the night. Jack and Neal probably pushed the limits further than ABL and his buddies, but their actions make me wonder if my lifelong wanderlust across every corner of our planet owes at least in part to the genes I inherited from this man. There are daily travel reports from New Orleans, Denver, El Paso, Chicago, Vincennes (Indiana), and a range of other destinations, large and small. Almost every card used the line, "I am feeling fine," which makes one wonder if he often felt bad. One of these told his mother that he was "having a wonderful trip. I had a good nite—feeling fine— it is 8:25 a.m. Leave here in ten minutes—Love to all—will write from Chicago—Bernard."

Some of his gentlest postcards are the ones sent to my aunt, his sister, Mary Scott. I knew Mary Scott for decades, and she only died a few years ago, at a very ripe old age. She was incredibly sweet and kind, living her whole life in rural Alabama, many decades of which were spent in the small town of Camden, where to this day, houses sell for far less than they do in most of the rest of the country. Her husband, John, was a stern, formalistic man who always scared me when I was in his imposing presence. Unfortunately, I never spoke to Mary Scott about her brother, ABL, but in-depth interviews with her son Larry uncovered quite a lot about his life.

In one card from 1924, he wrote, "Dear sugar, Be sweet and sometimes write to me. I sure do miss my little sister. B."

In another, also in 1924, he wrote, "Dearest sister, Are you feeling better by now? I do hope so. I don't want you to be sick while I am so far away. Write to me sometimes and tell me all the news. Love, Brother."

A decade or so later, he wrote, "Dearest honey, just a card this time to say that I was mighty glad to have had the few golden hours with you—all a few days ago—will write you a letter as soon as I have time. Love, Bunny."

The second batch of cards arrived not long after he left the South for good and settled into LA for his days at USC—and frequent

Venice Beach visits in 1924 and 1925. In them, he wrote lines such as, "Dearest Mother, I have had one wonderful time today. We have been everywhere. I will write you a letter and tell you all about it. We had fried chicken and everything. Love to all, Bernard."

"Dearest Mother, I am spending the weekend at Venice. I sure enjoy being down here. It is so restful. I am feeling fine. Write soon. All my love, Bernard."

"Dearest Mother, I didn't have time to write to you before I left the house. I am at school now. I didn't hear from you yesterday. I expect my letter today. We still have pretty weather, and I am getting along fine. Love, Bunny."

One card to his father was written initially as a question: "Did you have a good time in Indonesia? I guess you did. Be good and don't do anything I wouldn't. Bunny."

Toward the end of his college years, he wrote home again, this time to his mother, Pearl, using spelling techniques seemingly common for that time, where a space is included in words beginning with the prefix "to."

"Dearest Mother, I got through with work early to day, and I am now at home—Xmas is almost here for another time and almost another year—the time sure goes in a hurry these days. I had dinner with Lorene last nite, and I will again to nite—and will be with her to morrow—you see, she is taking mighty good care of me since you can't be here or me with you. I do hope you all will be well and happy this Xmas—and may the new year be a great success in every way to all of you. We will just try to do better from now on—than we have been in the past. Give all my love to everybody and spend a little Xmas cheer about for me—and take good care of your dear self and don't eat too much to morrow. Love, love and all my love, Bernard."

In another, written on June 3, 1928, he wrote, "This is my big day, and the day I have been waiting for, for a long time—I am mighty happy—but if you and Daddy were here I would be much happier—to day in about one hour—we line up for the Bacco services—this is a very beautiful affair—we also have the hooding exercise to day—Did you ever think I would graduate from a great university like this—

well, I am all through and tickled to death. It is all over—the only thing I regret is that you and Dad aren't here to see me finish—it's a great ole feeling to know that you are through. Lorene and her father are coming over this afternoon. I don't get my 'dip' until next Sat. That also will be a great day for your little Bernard—well, I must finish dressing now and go over to the university—Give my love to all and remember I love you dearly—Lorene, Bernard—P.S. I didn't go to church today. I stayed home and rested—this will be a long service to day."

In a letter to his mother after graduating from college, ABL proudly noted, "I was looking back over my college days today—you know, I have been pretty successful since I've been here—I will name the things I have been in—Trojan Squires, Trojan Knights (the little strips of paper tell the story), Bachelors' Club (member and president), Commerce Club, Varsity Club, mgr. Freshman Football, mgr. Freshman Track, asst. mgr. Varsity Football, asst. mgr. Varsity Track, mgr. Inter-Mural Sports, Alpha Kappa Psi—commerce prof. and Sigma Tau (social vice president and mgr. of House Paper '25–'26)"—busy boy that ABL. He was proud of himself too.

The clean-living and rather pious persona he created in many cards belies one of the seedier discoveries I have made during his university days and perhaps one of the most awful and revealing of all of his many sins; it involves his deep engagement with something called The Bachelors' Club. Reading through undated and untitled newspaper clippings that must stem from LA in the 1920s, during his days at USC, of course, I can sense the different era. The antics of what seems like a rather disgusting club took place during this time. But even The Roaring 20s and all that it stands for fall far short of making up for the excruciating misogyny and sexism that must have exuded from gatherings of this group.

One article was entitled, "Bachelors' Club to Stage Quest: Women Haters Will Meet at Red and Hanks to Pursue Elusive Prize" and informed the reader that the club "is an organization of SC male students who have distinguished themselves in campus activities." Another article published in a different paper on the same day, which lists my grandfather as one of the key members to be initiated, noted that the club is composed of the 'women haters' of the campus … [it is] a group of men predominantly active in campus life who have made themselves known by their antagonism toward the weaker sex. Some of the most well-known men of the campus are members of this organization." Appalling.

Oddly enough, it wasn't just this group of women haters that ABL was associated with. He also played a leading role in establishing a women's group, The Anti-Petting League. (He clearly had some unresolved issues.) A front-page article in the *Montgomery Journal* on March 26, 1926, contained a large photograph of ABL seemingly pulling a woman's arm, who is standing in line with seven other women ready to sign up for the league. ABL seems to be hamming it up for the camera and handwrote in pencil above the photograph, "By request of me, send it back will you, Earl," taking credit for the emergence of the league and its anti-petting pledges being established in Southern California. This league of "co-eds," a term common at the time at universities to describe women, was to be dedicated to ending "petting," with members committing to taking a pledge against petting. In language almost beyond belief, even considering the moralities of the day, an article said, "Girls are joining in droves—not the homely ones who couldn't find a petting partner anyway, but pretty girls, including many of the famed belles of the Southern California campus. And every girl, upon joining, must swear to observe the old-time restrictions on kissing and squeezing, i.e., she must kiss or squeeze and be kissed and squeezed by only a man to whom she has become engaged."

One of the adherents said, "And the movement will mean the doom of petting because girls not in college are deeply influenced by what the girls in college do."

When my grandfather left USC, he got his first professional job with the Retail Credit Card Company as an investigator. That term sounded much more significant than a credit card bill collector. His job was to track down those who hadn't paid their department store or car lot credit bills.

The head of the company was a lawyer who had helped these local companies write their credit applications and enforce their rules. ABL's job began with a phone call. He soon discarded the company's ineffective script. He tried to build relationships with delinquent customers. Being the sociable conversationalist he was, talking to strangers was no problem. It always began with a note of empathy: "I know these must be difficult times for you. You're not alone. Tell me what you're up against."

After gaining their confidence with his caring Southern gentleman persona, he'd begin to turn the screws. "You've got to understand an agreement is an agreement. Now, I can promise you, we're not going to send out the boys because I know you're going to take care of this." It was a technique that proved quite successful, and he was soon put onto bigger "scofflaws," as his boss referred to them.

He became a voracious reader of industry magazines. He wanted to see how others had figured out where and how to repossess goods that had gone well beyond delinquency. At one point, he even considered a detective job with the LAPD. His boss, an older man—gray and balding but for a fringe of hair and a bushy mustache that belied his loss of hair on top of his head—told him bluntly, "Don't be a fool, Leckie. In for a penny, in for a pound. You don't want to spend your life arresting drunks and lowlife, petty scofflaws. The money and fame comes by finding the real crooks."

It was just after he had made such a pronouncement that he tossed a magazine onto Leckie's desk touting the formation of the Department of Investigation (called the Department of Justice in those days).

ABL saw it as a calling filled with visions of the world's greatest detectives, a Hollywood movie he could not stop watching. The romance. The toughness. The manliness. He spent hours at the local library with the help of a gentleman librarian who had seen something different in the young Leckie. He introduced ABL to the world of the stacks and hidden information that had long been forgotten. The basement stacks had hidden nooks and crannies for inappropriate touches or close brush-bys, from which he may have never flinched.

After a few years with the credit card company, his boss told him if he truly wanted to advance in the Department of Investigation, ABL needed to find himself a wife. It was an idea, given his nature—and in light of his close encounters with the librarian—that he had never before considered. It wasn't that he hadn't dated women. He'd just never met the right one. Life wasn't always easy for a member of the Bachelor's Club, of course.

But in the fall of 1928, at the tender age of twenty-three, he married Lorene Kiesau, a very sweet and innocent young woman who was also a student at the time. They met at USC, and she was just right. And, as proof, just years later, my father, also called Bunny, was born.

ABL, having set the table, began the first course, applying to what was then simply called the Bureau of Investigation. All the boxes were checked and the criteria met. He had a wife, a son, and some valuable work experience as an investigator. He was ready for the big time.

It was never quite clear what drove my grandfather to choose this particular path. I suspect that if I had asked him why it was so important for him to join the Bureau, he would have told me, "To rid the world of evil. To do what is right."

What motivated this need, bordering on desperation, as he launched a full-fledged assault on becoming one of America's top cops? It was more than the conflicts of his ambiguous sexuality. The need to be the toughest guy. The smartest guy. The seductive nature of power and control. The romance of being handpicked for his courage, moral character, and incorruptibility. After having been touched one too many times, perhaps it was his latent desire to become one of the Untouchables. Perhaps he projected his own feelings of guilt onto others as a way of not feeling like he was enough. Maybe it was far more complex than that. There was something missing, and he knew exactly where he could find it.

While living at 449 No. Orlando in the Beverly Grove section of Los Angeles in 1934 (a house now valued at $1.7 million by Zillow.com), ABL could taste his desire to join the gang of G-men at the FBI. By 1934, he began his feverish campaign in earnest to work for what would become, a year later, the FBI. Clearly, ABL felt nothing short of desperate to work with this growing agency. By the end of the 1930s, the FBI had field offices in forty-two cities, employing 654 special agents and 1,141 support employees. But, in 1934, it was just getting started, and he wanted a piece of the action. Indeed, ABL would have done just about anything to join its ranks. I've accessed supportive letters from various fans sent to Hoover recommending ABL for a job as special agent with the FBI while he attended the Special Agents in Charge (SAC) School from June 10–25, 1934. Fueled by an ambition that overrode everything else, including his wife and small child, in a rather impressive effort at self-promotion, he arranged for scores of people he knew to write letters of support to the Bureau and Hoover. One of these, for instance, came from the vice president of the Farmers and Merchants National Bank. Among other things, language such as the following flowed from every letter: "I have had a personal acquaintance with Mr. Leckie over a period of several years, and by reason thereof, I believe him to be a young man of the highest moral integrity and quite capable as an investigator. Bespeaking your kind consideration on his behalf ..." I am doubtful that anyone else overwhelmed Hoover with as many letters of recommendation as ABL.

He understood the importance of what we now call networking. It had the right effect. The SAC School accepted him in June of 1934, a precursor to the FBI Academy that launched in Quantico, VA, five years later. He intensified his letter-writing campaign, gave talks, and spent his evenings—since Prohibition was a thing of the past by then—drinking with his friends well into the night. Hoover, struck by Leckie's dedication and ambition, sent H.H. Clegg, who played a prominent role in the founding of the FBI Academy, to do some due diligence on this eager and determined young applicant. Clegg, a Southerner himself, later became the assistant to the chancellor of the University of Mississippi, Ole Miss, where the civil rights entanglements strangling the South's unwillingness to carry out integration would catch him.

ABL received a letter confirming his wish to work for the agency, dated July 24, 1934, from Hoover himself, encouraging him to apply for the position of Special Agent. Clegg noted in his first of many due diligence reports that ABL "... has a good knack of meeting people, causing them to like him and then maintaining the contacts which he has thus developed. Without being unusually keen, he is yet shrewd. He is eager, ambitious, and conscientious. His lecture before the SAC School was not outstandingly good, and I have heard him do much better on other occasions. He perhaps was somewhat awed in the presence of authorities. However, I would judge him to possess average possibilities. Investigative ability—good; administrative ability—good; salesmanship—fair plus."

ABL formally applied to the FBI on September 1, 1934. Following a good performance at SAC School and those flowery letters, the FBI quickly appointed him as an administrative assistant to Hoover, having received a positive reply to his application from the director himself six days later. After so much work and preparation, his dreams of becoming a G-Man unfolded before his very eyes. He would have been glowing.

After this reply, E.P. Guinane initially interviewed ABL for a position on September 18, 1934. In the interview report, Guinane noted that, "Applicant is a free, easy talker and displays an excellent knowledge of his work. He has a pleasing personality, although not a particularly forceful personality. He impressed me as being mentally and physically alert and one who would be very thorough in his investigations."

Then, on September 27, 1934, Hoover requested a "very complete and thorough interview to be made in the community in which the applicant has been a resident and has probably had business and social dealings," indicating that the investigation should be completed by October 11, 1934. I scoured the many pages of the eventual interviews, fascinated not only by what it exposed about my mysterious granddad but also by how incredibly thorough it was. Recorded on October 3, 1934, the initial interview dealt with issues such as personal appearance, conduct during the interview, general intelligence, and information that revealed, among other things, that he liked to play golf. ABL was twenty-nine years old when the interview took place, and at the time—something that would change throughout his life— doctors deemed his health excellent and stated he had not experienced any serious illnesses. Dr. Vernon Stabler from Greenville advised "that Bernard drank a little but that he has never known him to be intoxicated." Another interviewee noted, "He is not addicted to strong liquor but does drink beer on occasion and that he does not gamble." He is "the best investigator in his line of work," according to Raymond Borden, vice president of a major national bank at the time.

Mr. J. South, principal of Butler County High School, Greenville, Alabama, stated that he had met Bernard and found his appearance to be striking. A fire destroyed the records of the high school in 1922, so Mr. South could only produce Bernard's senior year records, which reflected that Bernard was forn (misspelling in original) February 23, 1904 [incorrect date in original], he poorly attended, and that he passed chemistry, English, geometry, history, and social problems with an average of 76%—70% being passing. Note that his examination average in the above-mentioned subjects was 62%. Mr. South could not state any reasons for the attendance records.

Another entry into his review based on the views of J. J. Ferris noted that he considered ABL "one of the best students in high school, but while not a mental wizard, nevertheless he would get there, that he has good judgment, is a leader, active in school affairs, played football, that he always considered him honest, trustworthy, energetic, persistent, and reliable." Mr. Ferris advised that Bernard was a boy of clean habits and good morals and that his character was the best. His boss at Peagler Drugstore, Mr. W. S. Blackwell, said that "had never had a boy quite as good as Bernard ... he is well mannered, well poised, never loses his temper, makes a very good appearance, gets along well with people, is hard working, and is usually quiet, and that I consider him one of the finest young men I know and look for him to achieve something in life." Mr. Blackwell stated that he has known Bernard to drink a little, but that otherwise he was of good moral character and would make a good man for anyone.

One interviewee noted that "a Mr. Oscar Smith of Los Angeles put Bernard through college after he had made a lot of money in real estate promotion." Another stated that ABL was alert and quick to learn. Yet a third, J. Arthur Taylor, a vice president at Bank of America, said that ABL "has a host of friends and a fine personality, which enables him to obtain confidential information readily. He has good judgment; is discreet and is honest; and has a fine character of high ideals ... he had never heard of any scandal relative to applicant or of applicant's ever having been in trouble …." Another said he had a "fine personality and frank and manly appearance."

After interviewing over twenty people who knew ABL, Guinane concluded that, "I believe this participant would be of considerable value to the division and would probably develop into an executive." Interestingly, everyone else specifically mentions ABL's strong personality except this initial interviewer. Given what happened later, could this misread constitute the origins of everything that would go so tragically wrong?

Chapter 2

Into the Big Time: The FBI Years

John Edgar Hoover, the founder of the FBI, served as the hero figure in ABL's life. Hoover existed almost exclusively in the world of men. He viewed the world, in terms of gender and sex, through the lens of testosterone, brotherhood and maleness. But in terms of how he built and ran the FBI, author Beverly Gage reminds us that, "He also sought out men who would uphold the highest ideals of citizenship, refusing the temptations of alcohol, womanizing, bribery, even run-of-the-mill sloth. "I want the public to look upon the Bureau of Investigation of the Department of Justice as a group of gentlemen," he informed a national magazine, "and if the men here engaged can't conduct themselves in office as such, I will dismiss them."[7] People viewed Hoover as a man who sought out new employees as similar as possible to himself. If he liked them, promotions came speedily and with frequency. In this regard, ABL had a lot going for him. As 1934 made it past the halfway point, he took steps to become a G-Man: two White men from the South, smooth, dapper, and highly ambitious. They were

---

[7]Beverly Gage, *G-Man: J. Edgar Hoover and the Making of the American Century,* Viking, 2022, p. 112.

perfect for one another.

In his formal letter of accompanying his application to Hoover sent on September 1, 1934, following his initial interview in July of the same year, ABL writes, "For the past six and a half years I have been employed in the Los Angeles office of the Retail Credit Company of Atlanta, Georgia. My position with this concern has been that of investigator in the Los Angeles Metropolitan District. My work has primarily consisted of making character investigations in connection with Bond applications. I have become intensely interested in this field of endeavor and it is my desire to make this my life work. It is not my purpose to become a private detective or police officer of the common variety. I have contacted a number of men close to the Department and I am deeply impressed with the caliber of men in the service. Because of this and the fact that the Department is in no way controlled politically, I am submitting my application for your consideration."

As much as I know him now, I can see ABL going through the motions of an excited and aspiring employee to be. I can imagine that shortly after submitting his application, which he likely kissed and cuddled for good luck immediately before placing it gingerly into the mailbox, saying a little prayer, looking to the sky and hoping for the best, that ABL received an invitation to attend an interview with his hero himself, J. Edgar Hoover. The morning of the interview he probably awoke as a nervous wreck fearing rejection, failure, and everything this new town of Washington DC meant to him. The power, the subterfuge, all the attributes of city life and more temptations and vice than he had ever seen before even in LA. With abundant adrenalin flowing through his veins, he would have donned his finest suit, shined his shoes twice and plucked the dust particles from his favorite hat. Taking the rickety elevator down to the lobby from the 7th floor of the Hamilton Hotel he could taste both potential victory and loss at the very same time. He had given the process his all, but in the end, he knew it would always be a toss of the proverbial coin. He might be the ideal candidate to join the agency, but if Hoover – for whatever reason – didn't like him, he would have no chance.

He would have walked the several blocks to the Department of Justice as fast as he could, striding confidently inside, announcing himself and then waiting. After a few minutes someone escorted him upstairs to wait again, this time just outside of Hoover's office. There was a display case outside of Hoover's office displaying some of the mementos of their crime-fighting ways including possessions of criminals killed by agents which surely would have sent him into an ecstatic sense of awe. As ABL passed by the display case, he would have doubtlessly peered inside sighting the gold-rimmed eyeglasses of John Dillinger, the criminal who had terrorized the country for years, suddenly realizing the seriousness of this career decision. As he was eventually beckoned by a young secretary into Hoover's lair, a spark in her eye, with nervous energy overwhelming his abdomen, he would have stridden reluctantly into the hallowed ground of his hero. Inside he must have been shaking to the core, but outside I'm sure he tried his best to stand firm, stiff and as tall as he could unsure whether to shake the big man's hand, just wait for instructions or to sit down without permission.

Hoover probably looked him up and down, subtly at first but then with a growing sense of ease, perhaps falling just short of desire, and could have uttered "So Leckie, you want to work with us, do you? Tell me why." ABL, still unsure whether he should remain standing or sit down, continued to stand, and simply would have said something to the effect of "I have been waiting for this my whole life. It has always been my dream to work with the department and with you, in particular." A sly smile grew on Hoover's face, and he could have said something to the effect of "Sit down, relax, tell me more than all those letters you arranged to have sent on your behalf. In fact, tell me everything."

The interview must have gone as smoothly as possible. On July 24th, 1934, he received a letter from Hoover, himself. He didn't rip it open immediately. He held it tight, feeling his heart beating in anticipation. He knew his hard work: the letters, the meetings, his training, his sacrifices, were culminating in whatever he would find inside. Slowly, carefully, he tore the envelop open and pulled out the first of many letters he would ultimately receive from Hoover. It was everything he had dreamed. Hoover was encouraging him to apply for the position of Special Agent following his completion at the SAC

School.

On September 1, 1934, he sent off his formal application to the FBI and six days later, Hoover again replied personally welcoming him to the Bureau, informing him he would be interviewed by E.P. Guiname, who did so ten days later. During the interview process leading to his eventual hiring, the FBI conducted a series of role play tasks testing applicants in their interviewing skills. On one such occasion, ABL interviewed a person, based on which ABL wrote a report which he submitted to the Special Agents responsible for checking his credentials and skills. In the memo analyzing ABL's performance, Special Agent C.D. White writes on September 18, 1934, that "His manner of conducting the interview was highly intelligent, gentlemanly and tactful. I note, however, from the memorandum submitted by him to you that he has omitted considerable details with respect to the personalisms of Mr. Boyle as furnished by me. Most noticeable among these being drinking on the part of Mr. Boyle and a deformity of Mr. Boyle's right foot, described in detail to applicant."

Within a month, the agency appointed him to be Hoover's Administrative Assistant. Then on October 26, 1934, J. Edgar formally recommended hiring ABL as a Special Agent in the Division of Investigation, US Department of Justice at an annual salary of $2,900. With that, the wild ride that would unfold and engulf the life of this 29-year-old Alabama boy from Southern California had begun.

Hoover wrote a letter on October 30, 1934, instructing his staff to prepare letters formally appointing ABL and three others as Special Agents in the Division. He replied to the appointment letter Hoover wrote on November 3, 1934, accepting the terms four days later. Prior to that ABL sent a Western Union telegram to Hoover simply stating, "I accept appointment will be in Washington Nov Ninetheenth, A. Bernard Leckie." A letter was issued by Hoover on November 3 outlining his salary and the 5% reduction required under the *Economy Act of 1933*, a depression era measure designed to help repair the devastated economy following Wall Street's first major crash in October 1929.

I am trying to imagine the delight that ABL must have felt opening the letter, suddenly knowing that all that he had done to secure his employ with Hoover had borne fruit. All those letters, the schmoosing, the networking, the work experience and all the rest had paid off. He was no longer just an investigator for a credit agency in Los Angeles. He was a Special Agent, a G-Man. He had made it and his new life was about to begin.

He proceeded to Washington DC by the November 19, 1934, deadline, where he took the sacred investigator's oath. He arrived in the US capitol and booked into the Hamilton Hotel where he lived during his initial training between November 19, 1934 - January 26, 1935. There among other things, he received firearms training for pistols, shotguns, Thompson sub-machine guns, 30'06 bold action rifles, Colt monitor machine guns, and gas equipment. Once training was completed, with a score of 97%, they directed him to the Charlotte, North Carolina FBI office as a Special Agent. If a blurry newspaper photograph at the time is anything to judge him by, there he is proudly holding a small handgun, pensively yet proudly starring down the camera lens with his fellow training class at Quantico, Virginia in November 1934.

In a memo to Hoover's deputy Clyde Tolson (Hoover's alleged lifelong lover) dated February 2, 1935, a reviewer wrote the following concerns about ABL's training school performance, "He was lacking intact [sic] in certain interviews in the field but does have a saving quality of rather intense enthusiasm which, if properly directed, may serve the purpose of developing him into a Special Agent of average quality." In a subsequent Rating Sheet, the analyst notes that "His investigations in all instances have not been thorough, and he still requires rather close supervision. I feel, too, that he is slightly lacking in tact. This employee is possessed of an attractive personality, and makes excellent contacts." The issues of "tact" would come back and haunt him more than once in his future years.

One month later, on March 2, 1935, Special Agent A.B. Leckie's 30-day report noted that "unfortunately Agent Leckie is neither an accountant nor an attorney, and this affects him more than it does his work. He is unusually ambitious for a new agent and has an abundant supply of energy....he has asked to be assigned to overtime work during the weekends." His first case appears to have been the War

Risk Insurance case, and his first raise of $100 was made on May 8, 1935.

During his time at the FBI, the first substantive communication between Hoover and ABL was a letter dated June 25, 1935. ABL recommended that training schools should include courses of instruction on court procedures insofar as it affects agents. On September 9, 1935, he formally requested a transfer from Charlotte where he was posted first after his initial days in Washington DC to "some office much closer to the Pacific Coast" in a letter sent directly to Hoover. He received prompt approval to report for duty at the LA office on September 28, 1935. He stayed in LA for a couple of years before transferring back to DC and then to the Philadelphia FBI office where he spent both his brightest and darkest Bureau days.

During five years with the FBI, ABL was a widely sought-after public speaker, even though much of the work of FBI officials is carried out far from the public eye. He constantly addressed everything from large gatherings of law enforcement professionals to small events at grammar schools. After giving a speech to a school in Washington DC in 1937, the school administer wrote this to Hoover: "A.B. Leckie has come and gone, but we shall not soon forget the two splendid appearances he made here nor your kindness in sending him to us." In one of these speeches, covered in a local newspaper, he outlined what he saw as the Ten Commandments for Good Citizens that he suggested citizens should adopt in the fight against crime:

> 1. Be willing to serve on juries if called
> 2. Follow cases of convicted criminals to see that they serve their terms
> 3. Fight any connection between criminals and politicians
> 4. Be willing to testify in court if called
> 5. Make certain local police departments are equipped with modern arms to cope with criminals
> 6. Pay local police adequately
> 7. Vote at all elections
> 8. Discourage sympathy with those who broke the law
> 9. Organize boys' clubs and

10. Support discussions on crime prevention.

Not all that unreasonable. He loved his job.

Reviewing the many newspaper accounts of the different phases of ABL's life reveals the many sides and perhaps even more complexities of my grandfather's time on our planet. One thing that strikes me repeatedly is the frequency of factual and grammatical errors in so many of these publications. They would get the story right, but often not without distracting errors. In one of these, for instance, entitled *G-Man Talks at Assembly High School* incorrectly lists ABL as J. B. Leckie.

Very much like his grandson, often referred to by friends and colleagues as 'Stat Man' for his frequent retention and use of statistics to explain his worldviews, ABL cites a series of crime figures to stress the importance of the FBI and the G-Men. He notes that there were 1,500,000 crimes committed in 1936. Crimes were committed in more than one in every 16 homes that year. He proudly recounts the Bureau catching the majority of kidnapping gangs and criminals obtaining high-powered firearms by stealing from Government armouries.

Besides those nearly daily postcards during college, a fourth batch are postmarked from Washington DC during his FBI years. He sent most during the very first days in the Agency most likely after long days at work after returning to his room at the famous Hotel Hamilton, not far from the Department of Justice. This rectangular U-shaped building stood 11-stories high at the corner of 14th and K Streets. As one of the cards sent in November 1934 notes in the caption: "Hotel Hamilton – the only hotel selected by the jury of architects to receive the medal for structural beauty awarded by the Washington Board of Trade's Municipal Art Committee." On this card, ABL writes to his beloved mother, who everyone referred to as Momma Pearl, "Mother Dear – received your letter yesterday. Please don't worry about me – I am looking after myself in every way – be sweet and don't worry – I am well and OK – and work never hurt anyone. Love. Bernard." What a kind son.

As far as I have been able to discern, the first document still available where ABL proudly uses his new Special Agent moniker is a letter to Hoover dated January 4, 1935. In it, he gives a personal status report including his address, marital status, membership in social societies, including fraternities, and other basic data which he proudly signs: Very truly yours, A. Bernard Leckie, Special Agent. Just a week later another document reveals that ABL expressed a preference to be based at the Los Angeles office of the agency, presumably to be able to live with my grandmother and father. The Bureau briefly honored his request in 1936 and 1937, but the bulk of his FBI days were spent in DC, Charlotte, Philadelphia, Chicago, and New York. He again requested a transfer to the Los Angeles office in a letter of September 9, 1935, but they also rejected this request.

Six months into his FBI career an internal work performance report notes that he has "a very good personality, is rather sensitive, and lacks self-confidence." Another states yet again that ABL "is somewhat lacking in tact." However, just a few months later in a Special Efficiency Report by a boss that "I have rarely had the pleasure of working with a new Agent who displayed such interest and ambition in his work, and who has applied himself with such sustained energy and interest as has Agent Leckie. He voluntarily devotes many extra hours to his duties and is always prompt to volunteer his services on weekends, holidays, etc., if he is aware of any emergency matter pending in the office."

Hoover became increasingly impressed with ABL, as well. In a letter to the Head of the Los Angeles FBI Field Office, J. H. Hanson on August 18, 1936, Hoover notes "I was very favorably impressed with the appearance and bearing of Special Agent A. B. Leckie during an interview with him while he was attending the retraining school in Washington. It is my desire that you arrange to utilize the services of this agent in a supervisory capacity from time to time in order that the Bureau may be informed at an early date as to his aptitude for work of an executive or administrative nature." Almost a year after his second rejection of a request to move to LA, Hoover finally acceded to his request and ABL moved to LA playing a central role in surveillance in connection with the *Brekid* kidnapping case there in early 1936.

On February 20, 1937, he joined the Investigative Division where he worked on well known cases such as the famous *Mattson*

Kidnapping Case, the *Victims - White Slave Traffic Act Case*, the *Finch Murder Case*, the *Linda Mintz Case*, the *Tom Neal-Barbara Patpyton-Franchot Tome triangle*, the *Myford Irvine purported suicide*, and the *Walter Wanger shooting*. Up he rose through the ranks, step by step, reaching ever closer to the top, his dedication and enthusiasm paving the way for a lengthy career in his beloved FBI fighting crime and creating a safe and free society—or so he planned.

Following his move to Philadelphia to head the FBI office there, a poster for a local event proclaims: The Federal Bureau of Investigation entertains and instructs the next Poor Richard Luncheon Tuesday 19th in the person of Mr. A. B. Leckie, Philadelphia Department Head. While another exclaims "Listen to Our Tidings. All Men of the Parish are cordially invited to attend the May Meeting of the Men's Club of St. Paul's Episcopal Church, Guest Speaker Mr. Leckie, Chief of Philadelphia District for J. Edgar Hoover's Federal Bureau of Investigation Subject - The Crime Ledger, Wednesday, May 25th, 1938.

An article in the May 10, 1938, edition of the *Philadelphia Inquirer* includes the following quote: "Strides have been made by John Edgar Hoover, and the Federal Bureau of Investigation in advancing popular respect for law enforcement officers, but there is a long road to travel. A. Bernard Leckie, in the few months he has been FBI head in the Philadelphia area, has had more success in uniting all local law enforcement agencies than any of his predecessors. More power to his method! As of this writing, they're saying of him, "If you can't get along with Leckie, there's something the matter with YOU!" He might have lacked in tact, but he seems to have made up for it by being a rather likeable fellow.

While heading the FBI's Philadelphia office, he was invited in May 1939 to a dinner in honor of General Anastasio Somoza, then President of Nicaragua, by Davis Wilson, the Mayor of Philadelphia. Somoza's younger brother, Anastasio "Tachito" Somoza Debayle, went on to rule Nicaragua for decades with an iron fist and unyielding US support. His cruel and torture-laden dictatorial regime only ended after the late 1970s Sandinista uprising. The Sandinistas eventually took power in 1979 following an armed revolution as Somoza fled to

Paraguay where he was subsequently assassinated in 1980 by a seven-person hit squad sent from Managua.

Later that month, as war raged in much of the world, ABL wrote an article in *The Plan Monthly* magazine published by the Middle Atlantic Lumberman's Association called 'Better Homes Can Slow Down Crime'. He writes that "[e]very new low-cost home that shelters some family from the ravages of nature, also shelters them from the more serious ravages of crime....The more good homes to keep children off the streets, the better citizens we make and consequently there is less crime.....If we are to successfully combat the criminal army, we must prevent delinquencies in youth and must win them over to the side of law and order. There is no single factor that can do this job so effectively as a fine American home....We in the F.B.I. stand for "security...in the home....you lumbermen with your great heritage and power to do good must stand for 'security of the home'.''

He adds, "[i]t is this type of leadership that will build better homes, better homes that will certainly foster the new type of national idealism and respect for authority and the rights of others which I have already mentioned.....All honest citizens desiring the preservation of our American traditions for our future home-makers must dedicate themselves now to the eradicating from American thought the vicious, false modernism that 'Everything is all right as long as you can get away with it.' True progress in the war on crime starts in fine American homes. Build them. Make it possible for more and more people to own them and be assured we may look forward with pride towards a greater security for our loved ones....Thirty million homes hold the solution. If the younger generation is property trained and the proper examples set before it, the safety of tomorrow is assured....The American home holds the ultimate solution to our crime problem."

Finally, in a sentiment as valid in 1939 as it is today, ABL notes that "American Democracy as never before looms over the world's horizon as a beacon light of justice to all peoples. The very cornerstone of our social order is based upon the respect for the rights of others and adherence to the expressed will of the majority. We often say with pride that we live in a modern age. But every generation thought the same. Only one thing is truly modern – the traditional virtues of our heritage. Even they have been assailed by fly-by-night schemes and theories. Since the dawn of time adherence to certain rules of conduct has been fundamental. Laws of morality cannot be violated with impunity and neither can the laws of nature or of man. In times like these we must of course be prepared against foreign invasion, but at the same time we must not forget that the basic cause leading to the decline of all civilizations in the past had been debauchery of law and order. Let us abide by the truism of the ages and place first things first. The major task of society today is to insure [sic] that law and order shall reign supreme."

As someone dedicated to the enforcing the human right to adequate housing for everyone, everywhere for decades, this article staggered me. I have written literally hundreds of articles and books on precisely this issue; the human right to adequate housing. This right originates from the human rights principles in the United Nations Charter, perhaps the most important law in the world today. ABL, as we shall see, played an instrumental role in the meeting where the Charter was approved in San Francisco six years after he published his piece for the *Plan Monthly* linking crime to poor housing conditions. The Charter's articles 55 and 56 gave legal birth to the idea – so much taken for granted today by those who support them – that human rights existed for *individuals* everywhere. As humans we were no longer to be simply treated as objects of international law that concerned exclusively relations between and among nation states. Rather, people, individual persons, with the adoption of the Charter became *subjects* of international law—human rights law in particular.

This colossal conceptual leap further solidified three years later with the approval of the remarkable Universal Declaration on Human Rights (UDHR) on what happened to be my father's 16th birthday— something ABL must have surely celebrated somewhere in LA, on December 10, 1948. If we ever needed a global constitution, it would surely be the UDHR. As this document was spawned by the Charter, the thousands of treaties, frameworks, rules, resolutions, and comments that have emerged over the past 75 years have the Universal Declaration as their legal mother. I use and rely on the norms of this text daily, as I have throughout the decades spanning my life as an international human rights advocate across the board, always trying to push the boundaries of human rights law, winning such battles more often than I could have ever imagined—but never winning enough.

Three people drafted the UDHR's main components, including Eleanor Roosevelt, the wife of the longest serving US President FDR. The second was French legal scholar René Cassin, and the third was Canadian John Humphrey. It's difficult to describe the awe and honor I felt while strolling through the massive UN offices in Geneva—where all of the human rights activities took place in the mid-1980s—when I literally ran into John Humphrey in what was then called the UN Centre on Human Rights. I went straight up to him and said, "John Humphrey – you drafted the Universal Declaration! Can I please shake your hand?" Before I read the situation, I nervously thrust out my right hand to shake his hand and only then noticed that he was, literally, a one-armed man. At this point, he put his left hand forward towards me, I responded with mine and shook his hand, incredibly joyful to be in the presence of such an important person. He made a joke about his missing arm which I grinned at, which he used to write the first draft of the Declaration by hand all those decades before. He was an elderly man at that stage, but exuded a kindness, a hope and a care for humanity that is all too often missing in today's bifurcating world.

Another quote in ABL's article captures both the prevailing culture of the day and his worldview decades before, when he wrote "[o]f all the thousands of rogues who come before the eyes of the Federal Bureau of Investigation each day, there is only one characteristic common to each of them. They are all weaklings and cheats. The Al Bradys, Dillingers, Karpises, 'Baby Face' Nelsons, the Maises, Legurenzas', Bowers', and the thousands like them who chose crime as a career, all are puny weaklings who made of their lives a vicious habit of lies....Successful men learn to honor the rights of others. Lack of home discipline and healthy guidance, the lack of good low-cost homes to shelter growing children from the crowded atmosphere of slums, all too often lead to crime." You don't easily find a term of art that better captures an era as "puny weaklings!"

Beyond the hypocrisy of honoring the rights of others while simultaneously violating the rights of those with differing political views during his time in the House Un-American Activities Committee, I can't blame ABL for linking slums and crime. Unfortunately, this avowed bond remains widely held worldwide. As many political and perhaps other sins as he may have committed over the years – working for Hoover, spying on people without their permission, destroying people's lives in the McCarthy's Hollywood purges and his many other misdeeds, the more I understand ABL and learn of the intricate details of his life, the more I can see that at least in his mind, he was doing the right thing. He truly believed that he was making the world a better a place with more justice, less crime, and fewer people housed in destitute conditions. He tried in his way to build a better country—and indirectly a better world.

ABL spent several months in LA before transferring back to the DC office in February 1937. In a letter to headquarters, Special Agent in Charge J. H. Hanson advises that he inspected ABL's property, who was *en route* to Washington DC. He noted that everything was in good condition except for the .38 revolver, which has a chip in the wood grip. Besides the gun, ABL kept Americans safe from crime by carrying: 1 Leather pocket holster for .38 revolver, 1 leather shoulder holster for .38 revolver, 1 Colt Police Positive .38 revolver #411370, 1 badge # 284, 1 Commission Card #313 and case, 1 Manual of Instructions #69, 1 Manual of Rules & Regulations #696, 1 Agent's Brief Case, 1 Zipper Brief Case, 1 Digest of Decisions re National Banks, Vol. 1, 2, 3 & 4, and 1 U.S. Government Tax Exemption Identification Card #J-1406. The note includes reference to his annual leave status, indicating that ABL had 40 days and 30 minutes of accrued annual leave and 15 days accrued sick leave as of January 1937. Upon his return to Washington, he switched hotels and moved into the Lafayette Hotel, located on the corner of 16th and "I" Streets in the NW portion of the city.

ABL was out and about fighting crime during his FBI years. One article with the headline *G-Men Seize Kidnap Terrorist* also contains a profile photograph of ABL with the caption reading "A. Bernard Leckie, captured extort terrorist." In this case, the writer referred to as both as Morman and Moran as "a swarthy, stocky man of German extraction confessed and then wept incessantly." The article notes that

"Fearing the frenzied prisoner might attempt suicide, Leckie assigned a number of agents to guard him carefully and posted one man beside each window in the interrogation chamber." Moran developed a scheme, posing as a private detective who would secretly terrorize and extort wealthy families in the Philadelphia area, hoping they would hire him to discover who manipulated them. He did so, posing as a detective and a security guard, until he was captured after months of FBI investigation. His days as a criminal ended when "Finally Leckie and his men seized the suspect and he was grilled incessantly, breaking down and confessing that he had been responsible for the anguish he kept alive throughout the winter among his victims."

Also in his files, we find a life-sized target of a human body which ABL must have used for target practice with his .38. From this we can surmise that ABL consistently landed each bullet in either in the middle of the skull or directly on the sternum. Watch out bad guys!

The FOIA search provided a photocopy of one of the documents entitled *G-Men get G-men* (2-6-39) The article reads as follows: "Says Dress Salesman Posed as FBI Agent to Pass Bad Checks. A dress salesman accused of posing as an FBI operative and cashing several bad checks on the strength of his alleged connections, was held under $2500 bail for court today by the US Commissioner J. H. Molloy. A. Bernard Leckie, agent in charge of the Bureau of Investigation here, [Philadelphia] said Sidney Friedhaut, 23, Union st. near 40th and Girard av., identified himself to a number of persons as "Friedhaut, the G-Man." On one occasion he even displayed a telegram signed by J. E. H., intimating it was from J. Edgar Hoover, FBI head, complimenting him for work investigating "subversive activities of Nazis." The checks were cashed in several drug stores, and one was signed with Leckie's name he told the Commissioner."

As a driving characteristic, his blind ambition both served him and undermined him, sometimes all at once. He worked extremely long days, taking career risks that seemed like the right thing to do under the circumstances. Often those risks paid off. The FBI caught the criminals, enhancing Hoover, and ABL could stroll happily home after very long days at work. However, when things went awry, even if there was no attempt or intention, the consequences could be life changing. But before he learned these incredibly painful lessons, his aim was to be as close as possible with Hoover—and all that that implied.

Chapter 3

Cozying Up to Hoover

In the end, Hoover headed the FBI for forty-nine years, a term spanning the terms of many governments, both left and right, then ended his days at the head of the agency during the corrupt reign of the humiliated criminal President, Richard Nixon. As has been widely reported, Hoover, The Keeper of the Files, possessed dirt on all of America's leading politicians and influential personalities. I am certain he taught this technique to ABL. While we may never know how low ABL might have stooped to collect insalubrious stories, we certainly know that he kept files—hundreds of them. As I mentioned earlier, my father, having reviewed them following his father's sudden death, decided that their almost complete destruction was the only responsible course.

We also know for certain, of course, that Hoover's files were more than explosive. According to an article about Athan Theoharis, who wrote extensively on this issue, "Unlocking Hoover's files was a difficult task. He intended for all his files to remain secret forever and went to great lengths to shield them beneath layers of secrecy. He especially feared, for good reason, that the revelation of certain files would be extremely damaging to his reputation and went to even greater extremes to guarantee that these files would be secret forever. The file system he created consisted of mazes within mazes. He used tricky nomenclature and lies to hide his files, just as he may have used double *entendres* in letters to ABL many years after he ended his work at the FBI. The names of some parts of the system were especially strange. For instance, Theoharis discovered that one large segment of files carried the label "Do Not File." It contained files about particularly cruel operations, all of them illegal. Buried under the title, Theoharis found Hoover's Obscene File and Sex Deviates File, records of the intimate lives of members of Congress and other prominent people that he maintained for use as blackmail when a perceived need arose."[8]

In addition, we learn that "One of Theoharis's most alarming discoveries was the existence of the American Legion Contact Program. This program, like Hoover's national Black surveillance program that was revealed in the media files, resembled the massive surveillance conducted by the Stasi, East Germany's secret police. Through a secret formal agreement with the American Legion, 100,800 members of the organization's 16,700 posts regularly reported information from 1940–1966 to regional FBI officials about their fellow citizens. At first, the emphasis was on spying on people who worked in industrial plants. Later, it expanded into general political spying. Theoharis revealed this program in an article he wrote in 1985 in *Political Science Quarterly*."[9] While I have seen no specific evidence that ABL was a part of this program, his repeated work within industrial plants and his lifelong relationship with Hoover would seem reasonably strong evidence that this was the case.

In her recent book, Beverly Gage reminded us that many referred to Hoover as the most powerful man in 20th-century America: "If Hoover was most famous as a lawman, he was also known as a ruthless political warrior, unyielding to those who criticized him or tarnished his bureau's reputation."[10] She continued, stating that he

---

[8]Athan Theoharis Revealed J. Edgar Hoover's Secrets, in *The Nation*, 13 July 2021.
[9]Id.
[10]Supra, Gage, p. xii..

"emerged as one of history's great villains, perhaps the most universally reviled American political figure of the twentieth century. His abuses and excesses, from the secret manipulations of COINTELPRO to his deep-seated racism, offer a troubling case study in unaccountable government power … He also embodies conservative values ranging from anticommunism to White supremacy to a crusading and politicized interpretation of Christianity."[11] For a time, at least, ABL viewed this man as his hero which, by inference, reveals that ABL may have held some equally unpalatable views highly at odds with basic human rights principles.

Hoover obsessed over maintaining secrets: personal secrets, family secrets, organizational secrets, and the biggest secrets of all—the ones governments keep from their people—including crimes committed in their name. And yet, as secretive as he was, he was far less concerned when it came to private letters and cards. He wrote many such letters and cards to ABL, and ABL responded.

Perhaps the deeper origins of these letters and the rather close relationship of these men stemmed from elements of their lives that overlapped to remarkable degrees. Both of their families had personal secrets—Hoover's involved the collapse of a bank owned by his family, and ABL's among others, dubious allegiances to Confederate ways of thinking and all that that implies.

Beyond their years together at the FBI, Hoover and ABL shared many life qualities and preferences, including extremely close relationships with their mothers. Hoover lived with his mother for many years during his professional life, while ABL wrote constantly to his. Interestingly, Hoover's mother signed letters with the salutation "love + kisses," using precisely the same language on a handwritten postcard sent to ABL in the 1950s from someone named Johnny. Hoover often selected new employees on the basis of their membership in the Kappa Alpha fraternity—a racist entity founded in 1865 to preserve the cause of the White South. Similarly, when possible, he hired educated men from the South. While not a Kappa Alpha member, ABL belonged to another fraternity associated with

---

[11]Id, p. xiii.

horrible antics, a very White man who came very much from the South.

Gage noted that Hoover "also liked jokes and funny little ditties, especially those that seemed to evoke the secret world of adult men."[12] ABL enthusiastically enjoyed the very same type of risqué and bawdy humor, often hinting at gay sex. My father once showed me an unforgettable little business card-sized humorous card ABL used to carry around in his wallet, notable for its oddity and contents. One side of the card read: "Welcome to the Nudist Colony. Entrants must comply with the ten ground rules listed overleaf." Turning the card over, the prospective entrant to the clothes-less world had to agree to a range of things. I will never forget number nine on the card, which read, "During leapfrog games, Greeks must complete the jump." Make of that what you may.

Hoover was always favorably inclined towards those who played football, as well, which is yet another similarity. ABL played both high school and college football. Hoover and his lover Tolson also loved horse racing and attending the tracks on both the East and West Coasts, as did ABL and his son. His grandson loathed such venues and refused to attend them from a very young age, a view he continues to hold to this day.

Throughout his career, from beginning to end, Hoover obsessively attacked "radicalism" and "alien matters." He headed the newly formed Radical Division early on in the Justice Department. Hoover played a major and nefarious role in the famous Palmer Raids, which resulted in roundups and deportation of those deemed threatening, especially foreign-born radicals and communists. ABL's school essay on the "immigration problem" sadly echoes these sentiments with a high degree of consistency.

Again, even at the end of their lives, both Hoover's and ABL's paths converged in remarkable ways. Both Hoover and ABL kept secret files. Hoover's files were well-known and discussed widely to this day. ABL's remained undisclosed. I am certain he would have learned not only the mechanics of keeping files but also the power of

---

[12]Id, p. 22.

holding such valuable information. Potential press releases could alter the behavior of those threatened in a manner beneficial to the file holder. At the time of his death in 1972, Hoover held two sets of secret files in his office.

As Gage noted, "There were, in fact, two major sets of files in Hoover's office, materials that had been sequestered from the general system under his explicit instructions. The first was the Official & Confidential File, 164 folders containing information of such exquisite sensitivity that it was kept under lock and key in Hoover's filing cabinets ... The other collection consisted of what was known as the Personal File, papers of special significance for Hoover's private life rather than necessarily for the Bureau's business. Hoover had begun sorting through those folders in the months before his death, fearful that he would soon be forced to retire and lose control of their contents. He gave up quickly. Gandy [Hoover's longtime secretary] later insisted that the files consisted overwhelmingly of personal correspondence, 'letters from and to, and the original letters from, and the carbon of letters to personal friends.' Congressional investigators concluded, with good evidence, that official Bureau documents were in there as well. In either case, Gandy's next action constituted a painful loss for the historical record. Before his death, Hoover asked her to destroy the entire Personal File. She began carrying out his wishes on the day he died and continued for at least two months, tearing up each piece of paper before sending it along for shredding or incineration."[13]

As mentioned at the outset, from what my father said more than once, ABL kept over 250 immaculately kept secret files held in a locked filing cabinet. I am certain he learned this technique from his hero, J. Edgar. And, as with Hoover, ABL's files disappeared up in smoke right after his unceremonious death, although the decision to do so was made by my caring father who sought to protect reputations large and small, and not something that ABL had asked him to do upon his death.

Even down to the issue of body shape and size, Hoover and ABL

---

[13]Id, p. 720.

shared a tendency towards expanding girth as the years wore on. As Gage noted, "Hoover looked different at forty than he had a decade ago, when he bounded into the office as the trim, young director. He was thickening, his waist a few inches wider and softer, his face starting to acquire the heavy jowls that would eventually lead so many reporters to compare him to a bulldog."[14]

These and other similarities both brought these men together but also perhaps created a sense of familiarity so deep that it ended up breeding contempt. In mid-1938, the first of what became several disquieting reports on ABL's G-Man performance were issued. A memorandum for Mr. Tolson from Hoover, dated June 29, 1938, reads, "On June 25, I saw Special Agent in Charge A.B. Leckie, of the Philadelphia Office, who was attending the retraining class. Mr. Leckie conveys the impression of being thoroughly acquainted with his investigative work, and I believe if one can judge from his statements, that he probably 'runs' the Philadelphia office. In other words, there is no doubt in my mind that he dominates the investigative and administrative supervision of that office. He makes a favorable impression with the exception of having acquired, either knowingly or unknowingly, a pronounced poker expression. There seems to be a tendency on the part of a number of our executives to develop that rather blank plastic expression. Maybe this is supposed to be the 'dernier cri' [trendy], in investigative finesse, but frankly, I think it is undesirable, as it detracts from rather than adds to the personality of an individual."

A moving letter sent to ABL from an unnamed victim of an unidentified crime written on Friday, October 7, 1938, read: "Dear Mr. Leckie: [Redacted] joins me in extending to you and your men our deepest and most grateful thanks for the wonderful service you have rendered us in causing the arrest and conviction of [Redacted]. We, my husband, my children, and myself, can scarcely believe it possible that, once again, we are free to come and go as we please. During all these years, your agents have been most considerate and helpful, willing, at all times, to aid us in every way. Our deepest thanks also to [Redacted]

---

[14]Id. p. 172.

for his wonderful work. Again, Mr. Leckie, many, many thanks for making it possible for us to once more enjoy a peaceful life. Most sincerely, /signed/ [Redacted].

Another letter from Hoover to ABL on April 12, 1939, concerns a bank robbery. ABL neglected to obtain a search warrant during an investigation: the first instance where Hoover issued any sense of displeasure with ABL's otherwise admirable record. Hoover wrote, "The Bureau is displeased with the manner in which this investigation was handled by you, and it is desired that you call the attention of the agents involved in this investigation to the errors committed in order that a repetition of such errors may be avoided in the future. Very truly yours, John Edgar Hoover, director."

At the same time, an extremely detailed and heavily redacted nine-page internal memorandum for Director Hoover by James S. Egan was issued on June 19, 1939. It summarized an investigation led by ABL into an alleged leak of information from the Philadelphia FBI office, signalling trouble ahead. At the same time, Egan's investigative approach was clearly aggressive and unforgiving. At one point in the memo, he essentially accused ABL of fudging the truth in a formal statement he forced him to submit to. Egan noted, "This statement of Agent in Charge Leckie is attached, and I believe that it clearly indicates his lack of cooperation and loyalty, as well as his loquaciousness."

The disputed matter appears to be rather minor. ABL received news of his promotion to the Chicago office, and in confidence, shared this information with several subordinates. One of these employees, whose name is redacted from the documents, leaked this information outside the agency, and the media picked it up later that day. That unnamed agent was subsequently "relieved of his property" and presumably fired. But it wasn't just him, but ABL himself, who suffered greatly from these events.

The statement mentioned by Egan is a painful document to read. I can almost see my grandad squirming in his seat, trying not to admit to sharing confidential information, as Egan repeatedly asked pressing questions. At a certain point, Egan said, "Do you, at this time, realize the seriousness of giving out this information to agents and the information eventually getting out of the office?"

ABL replied with a placating answer designed for his tormentor, "I fully realize the seriousness of this matter, and so as far as I am concerned, there will never be a recurrence of a situation of this sort."

Just as the sweat must have started appearing on his brow, Egan continued, "Last night in your office, when I confronted Agent [Redacted] with Agent [Redacted] and Agent [Redacted] made the statement that he had no way of knowing of the transfers of Agents Clegg and Ladd, why didn't you inform me that you had told Agent [Redacted]?"

With sweat now assuredly pouring from his armpits and soaking his immaculate suit in the steamy summer air, in all likelihood ABL nervously and rather dubiously replied, "At the time, I did not remember that I had talked to him. It was only after considerable thought that I remembered exactly who I had talked to." Even to me this sounds rather fishy. I'm going to ask ABL about this the next time I speak to him in my dreams.

He was busted; that much is clear. He tried to hide discussing his transfer to Chicago—which again seems like a matter of paltry concern to the field of law enforcement—but clearly, within the world of Hoover, that qualified as a grave act of insubordination. Taking all else into account, this was the straw that broke the camel's back, forcing ABL to resign from his dream job, from his dream agency, working for his dream boss—just weeks later.

It is not immediately clear why such an infraction resulted in the following viciousness and venom, not only by Hoover and Tolson, in the end, but initially by Egan. In the penultimate paragraph of the lengthy memo, he wrote, "After the interviews were completed at Philadelphia, I definitely gained the opinion that the main trouble with SAC Leckie was that he had a 'swell head.' On Thursday night, on leaving the office at about eight, I walked toward the bus stop with him, and he informed me that the police dinner had turned into an almost testimonial for him and they had passed a long resolution endorsing his administration of the Philadelphia office, and he was really very concerned about it. I was surprised at this since he should know or realize what little value endorsements or resolutions of this kind amount to."

And yet, just days after Egan submitted his report, we find in the files a letter from Hoover to the journalist in Philadelphia who had come to learn of ABL's transfer to Chicago, Gary W. Bok. In it, Hoover noted, "I want you to know that I deeply appreciate your kind remarks concerning Mr. A.B. Leckie." Hoover responded to Bok's letter, which had been sent five days prior, where Bok expressed the viewpoint that "many of us here in Philadelphia are personally sorry to see Mr. Leckie leave this town, even though we are pleased that you felt him worthy of promotion. He has done an outstanding job in his regular work and, in addition, has made countless friends for your splendid organization through his knowledge of public relations."

Nevertheless, the first negative review of what had been a stellar rise did not have substantive consequences at the time. On May 13, 1939, ABL was promoted from $4,800 per annum to $5,000, as indicated in yet another letter from Hoover to him. Less than a month later, on June 3, he received notice from Hoover that he had been promoted again. He was directed to proceed to Chicago, America's second city, to assume the duties of special agent in charge of the Chicago Field Division. Promotion followed promotion, which, in turn, followed promotion. What could possibly have gone wrong?

ABL was clearly what the Germans call a *streber*, or an "ass kisser" or "brown-noser", and no one was more frequently a recipient of these attempts at being liked or loved than Hoover himself. ABL went to great lengths to ingratiate himself with the boss. In one letter, just a month after the first light rebuke on May 25, 1939, ABL sent Hoover the menu of an event called the G-Men Annual Reunion, where ABL planned to guest speak.

Interestingly, the letter continued, "On account of my attendance at the dinner given by the city of Philadelphia for President Anastasio Somoza of Nicaragua, I was late attending this meeting, but I did attend and speak to the members assembled for approximately five minutes." And he signed off using Hoover's traditional salutation: 'Very Truly Yours, A.B. Leckie, Special Agent in Charge.' As mentioned above, for anyone who is not familiar with the grotesque exploits of Somoza's son, read the history of Nicaragua in the 1950s–

1970s, and all will be revealed.

A message sent from the Department of Justice and the Northeastern Penitentiary in Lewisburg, Pennsylvania, in June 1939 indicated that the law enforcement community in Philadelphia was sad to see ABL moved to the higher profile office of Chicago. They expressed "genuine regret" about ABL's departure, even adding that, "I do not believe that I have ever known a man in any capacity who has made such inroads into the confidence of so many prominent people in a community as did Mr. Leckie, and I think it would be a pleasure to you to know of the warm spot that the people of Philadelphia District retain in their hearts for him. Such men are of tremendous value to your service and to the wonderful work that your bureau has accomplished."

A month later, ABL had apparently settled into his role in Chicago. On July 14, 1939, he received a letter from the chief of police of Chicago with a name extraordinarily close to the song title that began rock and roll, sung by Chuck Berry, John. G. Goode, addressed to "Barney."

Referencing ABL's presence at a police school graduation ceremony, Goode said, "Believe me, fellow, when I say your presence added color, tone, and dignity to that auspicious occasion."

Just over a month later, on August 16, 1939, a memo to Tolson from Hoover made it clear that everything was falling apart. In it, the director noted the following: "Mr. Foxworth telephoned from New York City and, after discussing other matters, stated that Special Agent Leckie came to him today and said he wanted to resign on August 24, 1939. He told Mr. Foxworth that he did not feel free to tell Mr. Foxworth just what he was going to do at this time but would write to me on Friday of this week to advise me exactly where he was going and what he was going to do. Mr. Leckie told Mr. Foxworth that he did not want the Bureau to get the idea that his resignation was because of the Philadelphia transfer, but it was due to his being offered a better position."

Oh really, Johnny? Is this really what happened? Having researched all the documents that cover the time period that I had access to, it is crystal clear that this is nothing more than classic institutional blather—in this case, between what so easily could have been closeted lovers who used homosexuality exposure of others as an eternal threat—putting "on the record" in the form of a memo, ideas that are clearly, for lack of a better word, fallacious. It is abundantly clear that Hoover and his cronies forced ABL out of the agency. I believe now, in my quest to understand the man I never met, that this singular event, which must have hit him like a speeding freight train at the tender age of thirty-five, may have pushed him from being a social drinker into the realms of daily inebriation and alcoholism, a practice that consumed him in later years.

Having fought so hard for so many years to build the career, track record, and support to get his foot into the door of his dream job by a man he almost saw as divine must have pierced him like the blade of a freshly sharpened dagger. Hoover fired countless agents he eventually determined were not the perfect G-Men he had once thought, so there is nothing unusual in the case of ABL facing a similar fate. But the face-saving allowance of resignation over the humiliation of termination did little to sugarcoat what must have been devastating for my poor old granddad.

Chapter 4

From Lap Dog to Kick Dog

And so it happened, with little warning or anticipation, *Mr. Favorite* almost overnight found himself becoming *Mr. Falling Out of Favor Fast*, a change that must have felt like a sudden body blow after preparing his entire life to become a G-Man and dreaming in more ways than one of a life close to G-Man Number One—Hoover. Suddenly, many decades before cancel culture was born, Bunny's one-time idol ghosted him—and, in the process, changed his world forever.

ABL must have known that "Hoover vowed to fire any agent caught drinking—not because he was 'a fanatic' on the question, he insisted, but because 'when a man becomes part of this bureau, he must conduct himself, both officially and unofficially, as to eliminate the slightest possibility of criticism.'"[15] ABL must have been amply aware that, despite how much he admired or even loved him, "Hoover was not a kind boss, nor did he wish to be ... He understood any deviation from policy as a personal insult, a sign of insufficient devotion to the job, and worse, insufficient loyalty to the director."[16]

---

[15]Id, p. 113.
[16]Id, pp. 120-121.

No matter what the rationale, the rapid moves up in the FBI hierarchy did not end the in-house harassment, and several short months later, ABL received another reprimand, almost immediately after arriving in Philadelphia, for his preventative actions aiming to stop a possible robbery after his office learned that robbers planned to target a bank in Lansdowne. In an internal memo dated December 10, 1938, (incidentally the 6th birthday of ABL's son), E.A. Tamm of the FBI noted, "SAC Leckie stated that he sent two agents to this bank and that the newspapers today carried a story to the effect the FBI was guarding that bank."

Tamm then sent another memo dated January 10, 1939, a month later, wherein he "pointed out [to ABL] that he had committed a stupid blunder in assigning agents to guard a bank with local authorities upon some tip that the bank was to be robbed ... Leckie stated that he understood the mistake, which he had made and would not do it again."

Then, yet again, some seven weeks later, in another humiliating letter dated May 16, 1939, Hoover wrote to ABL, "The April 25, 1939, issue of Lancaster, Pennsylvania's *The Intelligencer Journal*, in a news article regarding the address, which you made before the meeting of the Lancaster Junior Chamber of Commerce, quotes you as follows: 'Lancaster City has one of the most effective police units in the nation but the lousiest police station I have ever visited.' It would appear that you were quite extravagant in your praise, and the first portion of your statement is rather inconsistent with the last. Furthermore, it is felt that the reference 'lousiest police station' is not in keeping with the dignity of your office. Accordingly, it is believed that you should be a little more discreet in your public addresses, both in commending police departments and in criticizing their activities or facilities"—yet another take down that must have hit ABL hard.

This critique is somewhat at odds with Hoover's overall feelings toward police departments that "Though ostensibly a member of the law enforcement profession, he went out of his way to separate himself from ordinary policemen, whom he depicted as a cabal of corrupt, undereducated, easy-to-deceive thugs."[17]

It became clear that Hoover looked to oust ABL from the Bureau he loved so much, to which he had committed virtually every waking hour for years. But why? Were these relatively minor lapses so vital to the integrity and reputation of the FBI as to require termination, or could it have been something entirely different? Given the fact that ABL and Hoover continued to correspond *for more than two decades* after his unceremonious departure from the Bureau and their mutual involvement in a number of political and criminal matters during that time, it feels as if something else had to be up, but what? Micro-managing to protect institutional reputation is one thing, but this?

By 1939, ABL's annual salary had risen to five thousand dollars, after receiving raise after raise, almost doubling his starting pay in 1934. Then, in a letter from Hoover on June 3, 1939, the disgruntled director wanted ABL out of the Philadelphia office, shifting him unceremoniously to the Chicago office: "Dear Mr. Leckie: You are hereby directed to proceed to Chicago, Illinois, via Washington, DC, public business permitting, and assume the duties of special agent in charge of the Chicago Field Division. Very truly yours, John Edgar Hoover."

Just four days later, he had a change of heart, and things went pear-shaped again. On June 7, 1939, ABL was again chastised for being unreachable, with his whereabouts again being unknown. In a brutal memo just two days later, dated June 9, 1939, from Hoover to Tolson, he noted, "I telephoned Special Agent in Charge Leckie at Philadelphia this morning and severely reprimanded him for the leak, which had occurred in his office. I told him that his transfer to Chicago was canceled and that I would probably transfer him to the New York Office as one of the assistants to the agent in charge. Mr. Leckie stated that he realized that he was in error, and the only excuse he could offer was that he trusted people too far. I told him that this was no excuse for a man in an executive position in this bureau."

This resulted in ABL's relegation and a reduction in salary by 8%

---

[17]Id, p. 111.

down to $4,600. Hoover noted that ABL had committed a "dereliction of duty" and ordered him to move to the New York office by June 15, 1939. Things crumbled as ABL shuttled between new offices and cities every few days. Several days later, like a slow-motion train wreck with disaster as the only possible outcome, Hoover wrote (to my surely distraught grandfather), no longer even using his name: "Dear Sir: I have received Inspector Agan's [sic] report concerning the recent disclosure of confidential information in the Philadelphia Office. I am extremely displeased by your actions in this matter, and I trust there will be no repetition of similar conduct upon your part in the future."

And then, ABL and his allies must have arranged an attempt to defend him against the increasingly negative whims of his boss. Within three days, numerous letters in support of ABL began arriving on Hoover's desk, with lines such as, "A great many of us here in Philadelphia are personally sorry to see Mr. Leckie leave this town ..." The Police Chiefs Association of Philadelphia approved a resolution "with great regret," transferring ABL to another FBI office. He wasn't fired or forced to resign at that time. However, and in a memo from July 13, 1939, Hoover informed Tolson of an offer to ABL for the position of special agent in charge at the distant outpost of Honolulu. ABL preferred to remain in New York, where he had been recently transferred, after having first moved to Chicago, albeit very briefly. All these moves, of course, constituted serious demotions from the then higher-profile office in Philadelphia.

ABL's first four years in the FBI marked his heyday in the agency with regular promotions, a constant pattern of letter writing back and forth with Hoover, and involvement in major cases under investigation by the leading law enforcement agency in the country. He moved quickly from being just one of the boys to a place of respect, parting whatever groups of G-Men he would encounter along the narrow hallways of the Bureau, happily receiving envious looks because of how quickly he had become close to Hoover. He played a central role in some major arrests in cases involving murder, extortion, and kidnapping. He'd accepted repeated promotions to ever-higher positions of responsibility. However, in 1938, seemingly without warning, and with rather limited justification, things began changing for the worse. It all began with that letter in April 1938, where Hoover issued ABL with a stern reprimand for publicly mentioning cases involving spying when asked a question by a local reporter from the Associated Press. Apparently, ABL replied to the reporter that the Bureau had been involved in two prominent cases at the time: the Thompson and Farnsworth cases. He attempted to defend himself, replying, "No general information was given concerning the two cases mentioned above, but I thought in view of the fact that both matters had been definitely closed in the Bureau that I could cite them as an example of the type of cases handled by the Bureau," but his bosses' knives were out.

Then, as if seeking another reprimand, after four years without one, just three days later, his powerful boss harshly chastised ABL in a letter, noting that on April 4, 1938, "The Bureau endeavored for several hours to contact you by telephone through the Philadelphia office without success." In an April 12 response, ABL tried to wiggle out of the allegation. He noted that there was a mix-up; he attended a dinner, and it was wrongly assumed he was not to be disturbed. His boss shortly thereafter harangued him about the results of a urine test in May 1938. Then again, in July, he critiqued ABL for working overtime to the tune of fourteen hours a day, amounting to an average of 5.75 extra hours a day. His countless efforts to impress the boss seemingly backfired, bringing critique and humiliation to his increasingly exhausted body. Confusingly, his imperfect performance at this stage, however, does not seem to have affected the FBI leader's views of ABL too negatively. As noted, in November 1938, he was appointed as special agent in charge of the Philadelphia FBI office. Reprimand after reprimand didn't lead to the door but rather to a considerable promotion. Strange.

Again, this could have been honest support for someone Hoover seemed to believe in, but it could also have been a way to get him out of Washington, away from Johnny, and especially away from Tolson, who may have been suspicious of ABL from day one. No matter what the rationale, the rapid moves up in the FBI hierarchy did not end the in-house harassment. Several short months later, they reprimanded him again, almost immediately after his arrival in Philadelphia, for his preventative actions against the potential bank robbery in Lansdowne, PA.

Just two months later, things further worsened for ABL. He received a harsh, admonishing letter on March 25, 1939, from his dear Hoover concerning acquired information from a person ABL considered a confidential FBI informant. Hoover said the entire story was erroneous. The director angrily wrote, "Obviously, the receipt of misinformation of this kind places the Bureau in a most embarrassing situation, and in this particular instance, the Bureau took action of a rather decisive nature in connection with the data furnished by you, which action has placed the Bureau into a most embarrassing position because the information furnished by you was entirely erroneous. I must insist that you exercise greater care in furnishing material to the Bureau, and on any occasion when there is a reasonable doubt as to the accuracy of the information transmitted by you, you should so indicate." Ouch. Could that have been a set up?

"After all we've been through, me and Johnny," ABL must have thought, "How could he do this to me after all I've done for him, well, and with him?" Already known as a heavy drinker, this turning point made ABL's weekend behavior a feature of every weeknight too. Was he driven to drink by his hero and, worse yet, his hero's secret boyfriend? Bunny simply couldn't endure it. He had become a father a few short years before and barely knew his son, as he was gone so often. His marriage never took hold, as with each passing month, he spent more and more time away from home publicly fighting crime— and privately fighting the demons and taming the untamable shrews. Once the dust settled, ABL got back into gear and prepared for the next case, working together with the police department of Lancaster, Pennsylvania.

I can imagine it unfolding like this:

Upon arriving by train in Lancaster, ABL took a room in the best hotel the town had to offer. He settled in, unpacked his leather suitcase, and planned his days. After an hour, he walked down the two flights of stairs into the lobby and asked the colorfully dressed doorman to hail him a taxi. Off he rode in the oversized whitewalltired car to the imposing Lancaster Police HQ. Upon entering the building, and after having become used to the immaculate condition that Hoover insisted be in place at the Bureau, ABL shockingly encountered screaming arrestees, a trash-strewn waiting area, unkempt officers with un-ironed and even unwashed uniforms, and the general odor of the place, which reminded him too much of his days at the mess hall during his training at what would become Quantico. Later that night, in one of his countless speeches, he told the public he was taken aback.

As was his custom, he arrived far too early at the venue, the brand-new building of the Lion's Club of Lancaster. With more than an hour to burn, he most likely found the nearest bar and ordered two shots of Early Times to get his one-man party started. Ernie, the bartender of, well, Ernie's, gave this plump little sleuth a half-smile, half-smirk stare after hearing ABL's lingering Southern accent, wondering which side this strange customer's family had been on during the early 1860s. He had his suspicions but said nothing other than, "New to these parts? Staying or just passing through?"

ABL had looked at him with the stone-cold look that had safely guided him through his law enforcement and secret life so far and just said, "Just passing through, friend. Gimmie two more shots, will ya?"

Ernie handed him two shot glasses, full, and ABL downed them immediately. "Four down, four to go," he thought. Within just thirty minutes, ABL downed eight shots of his favorite libation. He felt it was time to go back to the hall and headline the event, as he had promised. Steadying himself against the early spring chill still in the air, he wound his way back to the Lion's Den, shook a few hands as he entered the full room, and hoped no one would smell the Early Times (which, of course, as always, they did). He made his way to the reserved seat in the front row with a little name plate announcing the speaker for the evening. He sat next to the chief of police and his wife. The woman smelled the whisky on his breath and immediately made googly eyes at the man from DC, whom she saw as a cute, badass power broker. Her flirty demeanor was no match for her husband's, however, and if Bunny had ever stared into "let's do it" eyes more determined than those of the chief, he was at a loss as to when that might have been. Power seeks power, they say, and these two sets of powerful eyes peered as deeply as four eyes could down the long tunnel of possibility that existed for two law enforcers in the mid-Depression, pre-war age of homophobia, secretly salivating at what could come later.

After an introduction that wowed the business-minded crowd who would attend a chamber of commerce meeting like that, ABL went to the lectern to tell the assembled about new crime-fighting techniques, new threats, and new moves afoot in Washington with FDR settled into year seven of what eventually were fourteen eventful years in the White House. ABL began his remarks with some not-so-subtle digs at FDR and the lefty New Deal, which he loathed. Then, as was his trademark, he made a series of bawdy jokes designed to lighten the atmosphere but which went down horribly. Having been unaware of the large percentage of Lancaster's police force having Greek roots, he repeated the tasteless joke about game rules at nudist camps: "In leapfrog games, Greeks must complete the jump." The speech went from bad to worse, and whatever charisma he thought he had seemed to drain from him with each passing second. When his talk turned to work, he began speaking about his visit earlier in the day to the police headquarters, thinking of the chief (and his abs) and praising the officers themselves but making countless references to the seedy atmosphere of the building itself. After the polite clapping by the fidgety and increasingly uncomfortable crowd, the event ended. Bunny headed back to Ernie's for a few more nightcaps, deluding himself into believing he'd done OK and could forget that night.

And then, in early August, ABL received an urgent memo from Hoover's secretary Della (who ABL would oddly marry decades later) to report to the director's office on August 7, promptly at 8 a.m. This would be anything but the seductively soothing meetings these two men had grown used to; something scary was clearly up. He would have arrived at 7:50 a.m., sat in the waiting area that had induced such awe five years earlier, and at precisely eight a.m., the secretary called him back.

We can imagine that ABL slowly entered the room. Hoover didn't even rise from his chair, merely motioning to ABL to sit down and await his admonishment. Not even a second after Bunny had sat down, Johnny could have exploded at his once close friend, yelling so loudly that it must have been heard far beyond the walls of his office. Given the contents of the all the recent memos, he could have shouted something to the effect of "What in the world were you thinking, idiot? It's over. You're out. Enough is enough. Only because you are you am I going to give you a chance to save face and will let you resign, but as far I am concerned, you are fired; you're out!" There were no words from the G-Man, his head instantly dropping lower than ever before, as if his neck muscles had suddenly disappeared altogether. The humiliation was complete. The despair was immeasurable. The depression was immediate.

At some point, ABL must have capitulated to the pressure of the repeated reprimands, seen the writing on the wall, and simply had enough. His official resignation letter reads as follows:

> My dear Mr. Hoover:
>
> I hereby submit my resignation as a special agent of the Federal Bureau of Investigation, and I would like to cease active duty at the close of business August 24, 1939.
>
> I want you to know that I have enjoyed my work with the FBI, and I am sincerely grateful to you for the opportunity that I have had to work for this fine organization under your able leadership. My loyalty to you and the FBI will never cease.
>
> For your information, I have accepted a position as superintendent of officers for the New York Society for the Prevention of Cruelty to Children, and I expect to take over my new duties on August 28.
>
> I wish you continued success in the great work you are doing. I want you to know that if I can ever be of any assistance whatsoever that you only need to call upon me.
>
> With kindest personal regards, I remain yours truly,
> AB Leckie (signed)

In a letter to ABL, dated August 22, 1939, Hoover wrote, "In accordance with your request, your resignation is being accepted effective at the close of business November 23, 1939, active duty to cease at the close of business August 24th."

As I try to understand the mind and soul of my grandfather more than sixty years after his premature demise, I allow feelings to emerge that must have been the same as his while writing the most difficult letter of his life. I imagine not just the immense humiliation he must have felt, especially when he obediently observed to Hoover, "My loyalty to you and the FBI will never cease" but also the anger about his forced resignation from the institutional home of the man who was well on his way to becoming one of the most powerful Americans in the 20th century. ABL loved rubbing elbows (and probably shoulders and other appendages too) with the rich and powerful. He must have known subconsciously, at least, that his departure would be something that would impact him to one degree or another throughout the remainder of his life.

According to an internal FBI report on ABL after his departure from the agency, ABL "wanted to give the feeling that he still had the director's friendship." His dream job with the FBI ended, and the police department of Philadelphia considered him for the position of chief of police. He declined when the mayor proposed this option to him, presumably feeling it was a position far beneath him. In a view completely at odds with his bosses in the Bureau, some of his former colleagues lauded him as the "most popular SAC ever in the Philadelphia office."

As is apparent from several of the internal FBI memos obtained through the FOIA search, the hard-handed treatment aimed at ABL didn't end with his employment there. Some months after leaving the agency, he spoke at another testimonial dinner, observed and reported on by a currently active agent. In a report on ABL, the agent noted that, "The address was delivered by former SAC Leckie, who was most obscene and uncouth in his remarks ... He then started telling some dirty stories, which fell flat."

ABL addressed the Philadelphia Police Chief's Association on September 14, 1939, right in between the end of his active duty for the

FBI and his formal date of resignation, an event also observed by the FBI. A connected report to Hoover noted that ABL "is still extremely popular with the officers of this association" and that "he paid a high and apparently sincere tribute to you and the Bureau, stating you would go down in history as the outstanding law enforcement officer of all time and that the Bureau, in his estimation, was the finest organization in the world. He stated that he held you and the Bureau in the highest esteem and that his reason for taking the above-mentioned job [Superintendent of the New York Society for the Prevention of Cruelty to Children] was entirely personal." In my estimation, he slightly over-did the flattery ...

After the meeting, Leckie immediately left, which conveyed the impression to him that he recognized the fact that he had made a fool of himself. It was obvious he had been drinking considerably, and he did not attend a private party that was given to [Redacted] afterward. SAC Harvey was very cold to Leckie, and the agents in the Philadelphia office who attended the dinner were very much upset over Leckie's actions, characterizing them as shockingly revolting and uncalled for ... I told Sears [FBI agent] that next Thursday night, or the next time he sees Leckie, he should tell him what a perfect fool he made of himself and ask him what he meant by making the statements that he did, which were both uncomplimentary to the Bureau and [Redacted]."

In handwritten comments on the memo, Hoover notoriously wrote, "Sears should mince no words with Leckie. Let him have it." This was simply signed "H." The highest echelons of power within the leading law enforcement agency in the most powerful country in the world instructed employees to threateningly *let him have it*. Determining exactly what "it" was turned out to be to this former employee, over whom Hoover should have held no sway when it was administered, remains a mystery and probably always will.

Hoover's support for the Hollywood film industry to prepare films supporting the FBI crucially raised the institution's profile, as well as his own. Hollywood produced a blockbuster film by Warner Brothers called *G-Men* which came out in April 1935, right as ABL was getting into his stride, himself a G-Man by then. In 1935 another FBI-themed film released was *Let 'Em Have It*, ironically the very same phrase Hoover himself used when admonishing ABL as his days with the Bureau came to an end—at least officially.

Just a year before, Hoover had referred explicitly to the testimonial dinner given *for* ABL on February 27, 1939, in a letter dated March 10, 1939, where he noted that, "I have just received a letter from Mr. Hamilton Dalton advising that he would send me a reprint of the cartoon which Jerry Doyle prepared, and I am looking forward to seeing it."

This is in reference to virtually the only thing I knew about my granddad growing up: that famous and eerie poster hanging in my dad's den with Hoover looming spookily above the submissive ABL. Hoover, deeply hypocritical in his actions, like a perfect Machiavellian, played both the good guy and the bad guy simultaneously—all perhaps part of a larger hidden plan. Three years later, after having publicly uttered, "Leckie is an outstanding agent ..." on July 28, 1942, Hoover wrote a letter in reply to an inquiry about his views on ABL obtaining employment with Consolidated Aircraft Corporation in San Diego. Pulling no punches, he stated, "Even though Mr. Leckie submitted his resignation voluntarily, I am sorry that, at the present time, I cannot recommend him for employment." ABL began the job before the letter arrived. Unfortunately, they summarily fired him after just two weeks, surely thanks in part to Hoover's unwillingness to support him.

In another memo dated October 29, 1942, written by L. R. Pennington to E. A. Tamm of the FBI concerning ABL, the memo's author noted that, "While in Los Angeles at the Peace Officers' Convention, I met the above former SAC. Mr. Leckie repeatedly reiterated the fact that he would give anything to be back in the Bureau and particularly asked that I express his regards to the director. Mr. Leckie feels he was the victim of circumstances in Philadelphia several years ago when premature information got out concerning the transfer of a number of SACs and wanted me to know that he had no hard feelings against anyone and wanted us to realize that despite the fact he resigned after his transfer to Chicago was canceled, he would still rather be in the Bureau than in his present occupation."

Then, out of the blue, a full twelve years after leaving the FBI, ABL received a letter from Hoover, where he formally noted, "Dear sir, Your letter of June 30, 1951, has been received and your denial of having furnished any confidential information to unauthorized persons has been made a matter of record in this Bureau. Your consideration in writing to me concerning the matter is very much appreciated."

Throughout his time at the FBI, Hoover offered ABL more than ten promotions. ABL received glowing work reports and was given ever-increasing amounts of responsibility, but despite this, the agency eventually forced him to resign. This must have devastated him and could certainly be something he found difficult to live with for the rest of his life. His resignation was, indeed, technically voluntary, but reviewing hundreds of internal FBI documents reveals that he was forced out by an increasingly angry Hoover (and equally disappointed, or perhaps threatened, Tolson) who issued rebuke after rebuke in quick succession during his final year with the agency—for a series of seemingly minor infringements.

In the end, ABL worked for five years and four days for the FBI, starting on November 19, 1934, and ending his tenure there on November 23, 1939. On August 22, 1939, the attorney general of the US wrote to ABL with the following message: "Your voluntary resignation as a special agent in the Federal Bureau of Investigation, Department of Justice, is hereby accepted, without prejudice, effective at the close of business November 23, 1939." And with that, ABL's days at the FBI—at least the official ones—were over and done.

Chapter 5

The War Years

After his unceremonious departure from the FBI, ABL stayed in New York, going on to become the superintendent of the New York Society for the Prevention of Cruelty to Children. In this short-lived role, ABL met with a range of child movie stars and arranged for signed publicity photos from Jane Withers with a handwritten note to my father, which read, "To Bunny—I think you have a swell daddy—Jane Withers" in a slightly different use of the word "swell" than had been used previously.

We have another signed photo from child star Shirley Temple to my dad, again arranged by his gregarious father, intended to impress and please. It seems likely that he probably met her through his engagement in an extortion case in which she was involved. His society work involved a number of public speeches outlining the importance of protecting children from crimes but equally from preventing kids from becoming criminals themselves. Reviewing a series of index cards for his speeches during this time, he noted that, "The most discouraging phase of the entire situation is the overwhelming participation of youth in criminal activities. The law enforcement profession knows that there are seven hundred thousand young boys and girls who have traded their chance for success and happiness for the filthy, sordid life of the underworld. Children who grow up in the splendid atmosphere of a good home and a good home life have no desire to go out of their homes to seek amusement and excitement elsewhere. If we are to successfully combat the criminal army, we must prevent delinquencies in youth and must win them over to the side of law and order."

One of the strangest discoveries I have made is the huge disconnect between ABL's sudden fall from grace at the FBI and the continued exchanges Hoover and he shared for *twenty-three more years* until ABL's death. One or two of these were adversarial, but the majority clearly were not. It could be me, but how often is it that a person squeezed out of his dream job by his former boss continues to stay in close contact with that very same boss for decades to come? Were these men closer than we know? Did Hoover perhaps maintain some sort of secret army of former agents and spies to do the dirty work that even his special agents could not risk carrying out themselves? Imagine something like G. Gordon Liddy's infamous Watergate Plumbers, that sort of arrangement, all in the interests of plausible deniability. Maybe Hoover asked ABL to spy on Marilyn Monroe during those final months of their lives. Perhaps something else entirely, or maybe both?

Shortly after he had started his new job in New York, my grandfather accepted a job with Lockheed Aircraft Corporation in 1940, with a salary of $4,800. He then became a US Navy lieutenant, serving in both New Jersey and Hawaii as a senior intelligence officer. In a letter from the corporation to ABL, they requested that he provide a birth certificate, referencing the views about Alabama by those living in California. In a tone reminiscent of the times, and eerily similar to sentiments so disturbingly present in the United States today as it slides headfirst into fascism in 2025, the letter noted that, "We employ only citizens, of course, and our native-born people must furnish birth certificates or the next best proof. Alabama is such a backward state (in fact, so much so that even you left there). I presume that you will not be able to find a birth certificate ... In case there was a 'mammy' in attendance at the delivery, you should get an affidavit from her, but be sure to get her fingerprint impression along with an 'X'-mark, as I know she won't be able to write." Wow.

ABL's posting to Hawaii, not yet a US State, occurred during World War II, which had already raged globally for over three brutal years with Nazi, Japanese, and Italian conquests before the US entered the war following the devastating attack on Pearl Harbor by Japanese planes on December 7, 1941. Despite rightfully being welcomed home as heroes for quashing genocide and fascism when the war finally ended in 1945, until late 1941, opposition within the US against entering the war was strong, led by conservative members of Congress with their early versions of America First, despite all the evidence of the brutality of the Nazis and other Axis powers around the world. This nationalistic, inward-looking streak remains very much alive and well in the US today, and elements of it have placed the country in an incredibly precarious position, with millions of people still blindly supporting a man seemingly intent on entrenching a fascist future in a country once the envy of the world.

Even as a non-violent, Buddhist-leaning man who loves all of humanity and views them all as equals, I believe it's clear that the US entry into World War II was justified. It may have taken them three years because of the right-wing views in the country at the time, but had they not entered, the world would have been a very different, and far worse, place. Those willing today to turn their backs on the illegal invasion of Ukraine by Russia, the ongoing genocide in Gaza perpetuated by the State of Israel and the countless other cruelties meted out across the world would be well advised to learn such vital historical lessons.

ABL remained in the Naval Reserve from at least 1938 onwards, although he requested leave in August 1941. It is not clear if the Navy granted this request. On December 23, 1942, ABL received a waiver of physical defect for appointment in the US Naval Reserve on the following health grounds: "Forty-three pounds over standard weight (height 69 1/2 inches—weight 201 pounds) with a protuberant abdomen." Yikes! He was reinstated in 1943 and remained at Pearl Harbor for the remainder of the war.

Over the years, some have alleged that the US government knew that the Japanese Air Force was approaching Hawaii and, seeking a pretext to enter the war, intentionally sent warnings to the Hawaiian base too late. This allowed the planes to attack, resulting in the deaths of hundreds of US soldiers and destroying huge chunks of the Pacific Fleet.[18] One day later, those favoring US engagement in the war got their wish. The US finally entered the war, where it, together with its allies, including the Soviet Union, ultimately destroyed the Nazis and other Axis Powers. I remember watching the filming of a feature film depicting these events in the 1970 film *Tora, Tora, Tora* along the beach in Southern California at some point in the late 1960s, having no idea that my granddad might have been working in intelligence in Hawaii when the Japanese attack took place. Given his extraordinary Gumpish-like proximity to so many world events and his former high profile within the FBI and intelligence communities, I wonder if he played any role in the events that unfolded at Pearl Harbor—or if it was simply a mere coincidence.

---

[18]See, for instance, George Victor, Review of "*The Pearl Harbor Myth: Rethinking the Unthinkable*" by Robert Higgs. *The Pearl Harbor Myth: Rethinking the Unthinkable*, (May 2008).

Chapter 6

Getting the United Nations Up and Running

Regardless of his role in Hawaii during the war and his less-than-ideal departure from the FBI, ABL clearly navigated his career effectively during the war. He was appointed as the Navy security chief for the UN Conference in San Francisco in 1945, where founding member countries worked tirelessly for two months to draft and adopt the UN Charter. Again, discovering that ABL was in the room when this founding document was drafted and approved sent shivers down my UN-loving spine. Of all the thousands of laws in the world, none surpasses the UN Charter in terms of importance for maintaining the international order we have chosen to organize ourselves around. Without the UN Charter and the extraordinary principles it enshrines, the world would be a far, far worse place than it is.

ABL received a certificate of satisfactory service from the secretary of the Navy, Artemus L. Gates, on that infamous day, August 6, 1945, when the same military of which he was an integral part killed more than one hundred thousand civilians with the first-ever atomic weapon dropped onto Hiroshima. I haven't been able to figure out precisely what day-to-day role ABL played during the UN Conference on International Organisation in San Francisco, held for two vital months from April 25–June 26, 1945. However, that he was there at all is deeply meaningful to me. I have spent my entire career breathing as much life as possible into the Charter and all the numerous international law standards to which this cornerstone document eventually gave birth.

ABL, an intelligence officer with years of FBI and investigative experience was appointed as Navy security chief to the inaugural meeting of what became the UN. This global gathering, where it is widely alleged that the hosts, the United States, secretly spied on every single delegation, including allies, certainly raises the potential that ABL himself, the rotund right-winger from the deep South, protuberant abdomen and all, carried out espionage on visiting diplomatic delegations. This could have influenced the final outcome of the gathering and beyond.[19]

In one of his very few remaining files, there is a red-covered, almost pristine advance copy of the "Who's Who—Delegates to the UN Conference on International Organization, San Francisco 1945," on which someone has written in pencil, "Mark Hopkins Desk Copy—Conference Information Desk—Do Not Remove." ABL apparently ignored the message, removed it, and now this historic booklet sits snugly in my office files. Sorry, Mr. Hopkins. It contains the résumés of all the delegates from the forty-six countries represented at this monumentally important gathering. Inside the front cover, ABL taped invitations to two cocktail receptions hosted by various delegations, which I'm sure he must have attended, given his love of all things libational, as well as his daily ticket to the San Francisco Opera House, where lawmakers drafted and finally approved the document that holds the world together.

I have spent many years' worth of working days running around the corridors and meeting rooms of the UN, working as an expert advisor to the UN in dozens of countries across the world. To say that

---

[19]Stephan C. Schleinger's book *The Act of Creation: The Founding of the United Nations – A Story of Superpowers, Secret Agents, Wartime Allies, and Enemies, and Their Quest for a Peaceful World* (Westview, 2003) provides a fascinating and detailed overview of just how pervasive US spying was prior to and during the process leading to the adoption of the UN Charter.

I am familiar with what goes on in diplomatic settings and how things get done would, in all modesty, be a great understatement. From 1991–2005, I spent months every year at the UN buildings in Geneva, where the UN carries out most of its human rights work. I drafted more than one hundred UN resolutions and other documents that expert and political bodies approved, on issues ranging from prohibiting forced evictions, securing housing rights, restoring property rights to refugees and internally displaced persons, getting climate displacement issues onto the international agenda, and so on. In my ongoing advocacy efforts on behalf of some of the world's most vulnerable people, I utilize the UN as a vehicle through which justice can be sought, through which compassion for strangers could take on a tangible form —the very same UN that my grandfather helped to bring to life in San Francisco in the mid-1940s.

Indicative of the times and the progress since then, of the 267 delegates listed in the document, a mere five are women. The UN Charter—written and approved by a voting pool of delegates—the world's most important law—was thus—perhaps unsurprising given history, yet alarming—comprised itself of 98% men and 2% women. This cornerstone document that forms the very foundations of the entire international legal order as it exists today was a sacred agreement made by men, for men, and of men. It continues to be a document all too often ignored by, opposed by, and violated by men— sometimes women but mostly men. How might it have differed if women were given their fair share of input? One can only speculate. Maybe the Security Council veto would have never come into effect. Perhaps the UN General Assembly resolutions would be universally legally binding and treated as such. Conceivably, the UNGA could have become a people's body comprised of citizen delegates, much closer to the wildly discussed idea of a global parliament at the time, grounded in the promising opening words of the UN Charter, which begins with, "We the peoples of the UN ..." Maybe the use of force would have been regulated more vigorously and military bases by foreign powers in other countries banned. Possibly, governments could have established an international police and military force to enforce the principles of the charter. Maybe UN peacekeepers, rather than soldiers from the more powerful countries, could have served in bases around the world as yet another deterrent to prevent war. Perhaps nuclear weapons could have been universally prohibited. So many things, including the history of the past eight decades, might have been so very different had women played a proportionate role as half of humanity in drafting the Charter. The possibilities of what could have been, as always, are endless.

And, as I recall my busy UN days—thankful now that I only rarely return—I imagine the moment-by-moment displays of power, ego, and sexual tension that would have oozed through the meeting rooms and hallways of the Opera House in 1945. Yes, the hugely disproportionate ratio of males to females at the founding meeting of the UN—49:1— probably meant that the normally highly sexually charged environment that seems to be ever-present at the UN was perhaps less than usual. At the same time, perhaps for those men who loved men, it was a field day, a giant cruise in the town where cruising became famous down Castro Street and beyond. If ABL had been so inclined, how did he spend his months there snooping around, spying on delegations, and pretending to provide security when surrounded by all those exotic men? One can only imagine.

One day, I may write another book solely about the role that sex and sexuality play not just at the UN but within all political and decision-making institutions. There are many horrible stories of sexual coercion and worse within parliaments worldwide, sadly recounted in newspapers. A particularly unpalatable gay Australian diplomat, who used to boast that he would masturbate in the UN toilets at least three times a day, every day, sexually victimized me. A gruesome Asian diplomat threatened a girlfriend of mine with rape, and a well-known Arab delegate nearly raped her—during what was meant to be a work meeting. On another occasion, a major European legal expert propositioned her, saying he would vote for a resolution if she joined him for a weekend away in Provence. If not, he would vote no. An employee at an organization I led was followed out of an elevator, then attacked in the underground tunnels of the Palais des Nations—where the UN is housed in Geneva. Horrible. And I am barely getting started. It is not always a safe place.

What most people will never read about, however, are the sexual exploits of men and women, straight and gay, that go on daily within the corridors of power, including the UN. I know at least twenty people who have absolutely had sex inside the UN headquarters buildings in New York and Geneva. I, myself, fell madly in love with a Swedish lawyer inside that building, a love that has lasted a lifetime. One time, I watched as two leading NGO activists were so aroused that they literally ran out of the building, hid—not very well—behind a tree, and made love while the rest of us made speeches and lobbied for our various issues. One time, sitting on the huge parklands that surround this, Europe's largest building, eating lunch with a bunch of Palestinian human rights lawyers, a wasp flew into the dress of a Dutch woman sitting with us. She did the only thing she could to get this evil little yellow pest away from her skin, ripping off her dress and standing there bra-less—in just her underwear—with the shocked Palestinians staring in wonder. Many high-ranking UN officials use the top of their desks as temporary beds. Tales of security camera footage of big shots and willing girlfriends making love on couches where their colleagues had sat just a few hours earlier. I could go on and on, but suffice it to say, when people are all squeezed into rooms for weeks on end, alcohol never far away, sleeping all too rarely, and working far too hard, it is not all that surprising that these things happen as often as they do. What may have happened in the Opera House remains to be seen.

In exploring ABL's role in San Francisco, I came across a rather tattered but still intact twenty-two-page "Program of the Closing Plenary Session" of the conference in ABL's files. It contains the full texts of the final speeches of major leaders at the time. There's an interesting statement from Andre Gromyko, who went on to play a major diplomatic role in the Soviet Union for decades during the Cold War to come before its demise, the unsettling remarks of Jan Smuts of apartheid South Africa before its long overdue dismantling in 1994, and many others.

Then there is President Harry S. Truman's speech, placed at the beginning of the document, just over two months before ordering the use of atomic weapons against civilians in Japan, speaking about the importance of the new UN Charter, saying that "It was the hope of such a charter that helped sustain the courage of stricken peoples through the darkest days of the war. For it is a declaration of great faith by the nations of the Earth-faith that war is not inevitable, faith that peace can be maintained."

I wonder what the soon-to-be-dead hundreds of thousands in Japan took away from these sentiments? And what of the millions who subsequently perished in Vietnam, Cambodia, Laos, Iraq, Afghanistan, Panama, Dominican Republic, Guatemala, Grenada, Nicaragua, Chile, and elsewhere during illegal US invasions and military coups supported by them since 1945? What about its repeated hypocritical support for dictators, occupying powers, and other authoritarian regimes, all contrary to the principles of the Charter the US pridefully designed and brought to fruition? The US's ongoing failure to ratify the Statute of the International Criminal Court and central human rights treaties, such as the International Covenant on Economic, Social, and Cultural Rights, reduces its credibility even when it does the right thing, such as forcefully opposing the illegal invasion of Ukraine by Russia in February 2022. How did these countries on the receiving end of US power feel about Truman's faith in the maintenance of peace and the eventual placement of some eight hundred US military bases throughout the world, which remain in place today?[20]

Whatever the exact nature of ABL's work in San Francisco, he received a certificate signed by the secretary general of the meeting, Alger Hiss. It acknowledged that as a member of the International Secretariat of the UN Conference, he had faithfully and diligently performed his duties, making a personal contribution to this historic event. Hiss, a US diplomat in charge of the San Francisco meeting, was later accused in 1948 of spying for the Soviet Union in the 1930s and found guilty of perjury, resulting in nearly four years of imprisonment.[21] I again wonder to this day what role ABL might have played in this infamous saga. Spies do stick sometimes together, but

---

[20]See David Vine, *Base Nation: How US Military Bases Abroad Harm America and the World*, Metropolitan Books, 2015.

they are also prone to tattle. So, who knows? Was ABL, too, some sort of double agent? He still corresponded with Hoover six years after his unceremonious removal from the FBI, as he began work for Joseph McCarthy and the House Un-American Activities Committee (HUAC). Not long after, he started his private eye business in Hollywood, so clearly leaning far more right than left, but in those frenetic years, I suppose, anything was possible.

Following ABL's work at the San Francisco meeting founding the UN, ABL received a letter of thanks from US congressman Karl Stefan, dated June 20, 1945. The letter reads, "Dear Lieutenant Lecki (misspelling in original), just a note to tell you of my deep appreciation to you for your kindness to me and Mrs. Stefan during our work in connection with the UN Conference at San Francisco …"

During his stay spying on government delegations from around the world, all under the guise of "security," ABL sent a little pocketbook of photos from San Francisco called "Views of San Francisco: The Bridges, Golden Gate Park, Cliff House, Chinatown, Etc." to his nephew, Lawrence, the son of his sister Mary Scott Godbold, after whom I was named. On the cover, in his own cursive handwriting, ABL wrote, "Dear Lawrence—This is a fine city—hope you can see it someday—Love to all—Uncle B." The famous city hall appears on the front cover and an image of the Bay Bridge and the skyline from the 1940s is visible in the foreground. Inside are photographs of all of San Francisco's tourist sites—the cable cars, Fisherman's Wharf, Coit Tower, Golden Gate Park, and elsewhere. There is even a picture of the Municipal Opera House nestled in the middle of these tattered pages, the very building where the UN Charter was conceived and ABL got up to his nefarious deeds.

From the front entrance of the Opera House, as ABL exited this historic building after another day of snooping as the fog rolled in during the late afternoon, he could have looked to his left across the

---

[21]Hiss, of course, strongly denied the allegations, and he recounts, in his own words, strongly and convincingly outlining the spurious nature of his conviction for perjury following imprisonment of 44 months in Griffin Fariello, *Red Scare: Memories of the American Inquisition - An Oral History by Griffin Fariello*, Avon Books, 1995. pp. 146-152 (Alger Hiss).

corner of the civic center and seen the civic auditorium, a place of history for the world, for San Francisco, and for me. Just over thirty-eight years after, ABL might have glanced at this spectacle of a building as the grandson he never met, a young and bright-eyed Scott Leckie, began a journey—perhaps stronger now than ever—watching his first live Grateful Dead show on December 29, 1983, instantly becoming a Deadhead, a status he proudly retains to this day. Little did I know at the time, ABL had worked just meters away less than four decades earlier; even less did I know at the time that *the* cornerstone international law of the 20th century was approved just steps from the entrance of a place where magical music spread through the air. The fact that I subsequently wrote dozens of international rules, guidelines, resolutions, general comments, and other laws during my career as an international human rights activist across the world, all of which were derived ultimately from the UN Charter itself, ties up these unusual links just a little tighter.

This tiny but significant corner of downtown in one of the world's great cities—despite its serious social pains today—reveals the extreme juxtaposition between my grandfather and me. Superficially, the differences may not appear as dramatic as they are in reality. But when you consider ABL's spying role during the meeting that led to the UN Charter and my life as a US-citizenship renouncing, lifelong expatriate, human rights advocate who ingested strange substances before Dead shows just steps away from where he sleuthed, it says much about my mixed feelings in uncovering my granddad's life and my efforts to repair some of the damage he and his coterie caused.

In fact, when I think back on the many hours that I spent lingering in front of what is now called the Bill Graham Auditorium in the mid-1980s before my permanent departure from the country of my birth in 1985, two of life's "That was the last time I ..." moments took place, more or less simultaneously. On the night before New Year's Eve in 1984 going into 1985, I visited the inside of a McDonald's for the very last time, purchasing a rather horrible cup of coffee just to stay awake after so many consecutive days of Deadheading. After nearly getting mugged on a quiet street between the Golden Arches and the front of the arena, I stood in hyper-energetic anticipation of the music to come, with my hippy girlfriend at the time, when a quintessential Deadhead guy, patchouli emanating from every pore, never-been-combed long hair drenching his head, came up to us. This very hairy stranger, as friendly as can be, tripping his mind out on some very strong acid, looked me straight in the eye and very enthusiastically said, "You know why you're here, and she knows why she's here. I know why I'm here, and everyone knows why we are …"

To which I could only reply, "Well, well, well, it seems like you're having a rather good time, my man."

"I sure am, brother. Want to join me?"

Having no other option than to do anything other than concur, I simply said, "Sure do."

He motioned to me to lift the lid on that horrendous cup of coffee, then proceeded to not drip a drop or two—or even sprinkle a small amount of this magical remedy into my coffee—but rather squirted a very large amount of mystical liquid from a Visine bottle straight into the squeaky white and yellow styrofoam cup. It was not the initial time that I had decided to consume this particular substance and explore the limitless inner void; but it was the only time I acquired it from a stranger in an excessive quantity. Those days, and especially at a Dead show, trust was ever-present, and while the experience was certainly memorable decades later, the liquid delight turned out to be tainted with some form of speed, which meant that neither of us could sleep until late in the afternoon the next day. Somehow, I don't think ABL could have related.

Uncovering so many elements of his life six decades after his death, my grandad was clearly the consummate patriotic American. His dedication to Hoover and the FBI during the 1930s and his work for McCarthy in the 1940s—two of America's darkest periods of human rights abuses committed against Americans themselves— embodied this as much as anything else he did. Though he did travel to several neighboring countries, mostly in the Caribbean, something not all that common during that time of his life, he felt intense pride about his country. He remained convinced that spying on and investigating people's secrets made America safe.

When we look at America today, particularly from the vantage points of other parts of the world where the rest of the 95.5% of world lives, it is ironic that what is now called patriotic in the US is advocated by extremist flag-waving right-wing fanatics tied to the rhetoric of a corrupt, aspiring dictator president. These insular, nationalistic individuals with so little to live for that they angrily displace the tragedy of their own failures onto others and instead of seeing what government can and should do for them, instead seek to dismantle the very institutions that patriots of an earlier era sought to build as bulwarks against the fascism the US had fought so hard against in the 1940s.

Chapter 7

Commie Hunting in Hollywood

Throughout ABL's career, while he may have accepted the inevitability of racial integration in the US—clearly influenced by the subtler ways of both the West and East Coasts, he unquestionably held conservative views close to Hoover's sentiments. After his time at the founding of the UN, he shifted gears and returned to his former job as a plant protection official at Lockheed in late 1945, continuing working there until he established his own business as an investigator in 1947, right as he was beginning his life as a private eye.

Hoover, along with a whole host of US political figures and the American population at large, was strongly anti-communist. This must have rubbed off on ABL quite considerably.[22] Though they shared the

---

[22]Hoover wrote a book about these matters, which is required reading if one wishes to know how the mind of the bulldog worked in practice: J. Edgar Hoover, *Masters of Deceit: The Story of Communism in America and How to Fight It*, Pocket Books Inc., 1958. As Gage noted, Hoover "believed in the power of the federal government to do great things and fight great battles on behalf of the nation's citizens. He also believed that there were certain groups—communists and racial minorities, above all —who threatened that project. His career reflected both themes: a faith in progressive, expert-driven government and a commitment to an avenging social

same disdain for left-wing politics, Hoover had a very competitive relationship with McCarthy of HUAC fame, often resulting in confusing but often simultaneously supportive and antagonistic approaches to McCarthy's committee. ABL happily joined forces with authoritarian right-wing politicians, a practice that culminated in his years of work as a lead investigator in Joseph McCarthy's odious HUAC, where he played a major role in hounding and spying on Hollywood celebrities allegedly partial to the US Communist Party.

The post-war fervor that led to the oppressive role played by the HUAC began in 1947 with a massive national screening program labeled the Loyalty Order, which involved background checks on more than five million federal workers and aspiring applicants. Among others, the FBI carried out extensive investigations of anyone thought to be either a broadly defined radical or, even worse, a communist.[23]

Communism terrified America at the time. Many were convinced that these "creepy leftists" had infiltrated all levels of government and society—just waiting for their chance to foment a workers' revolution in the heart of global capitalism.[24] According to Larry Tye, "In Hollywood, studio bosses put out word they wouldn't knowingly hire communist actors, screenwriters, directors, or musicians; later, to ensure they didn't make a mistake, they consulted *Red Channels*, a broadcast industry blacklist published by anti-Red stalwarts."[25]

---

conservatism. His genius came in amassing enough power to promote and enforce those ideas as he saw fit. Source: Supra, Gage, p. xi.

[23]Larry Tye, *Demagogue: The Life and Long Shadow of Senator Joe McCarthy*, Mariner Books, 2020, p. 132.

[24]Id, p. 133: ""… the attorney general prepared a list of subversive organizations that started with eighty-two, grew to 299, and included the Jewish Culture Society and United Negro and Allied Veterans of America. While it painted with a broad-brush groups supposedly sympathetic to communism—nobody explained why such sympathy was a threat when the Communist Party was legal—the ledger was then used more than anyone else, Joe McCarthy, to crush the groups and anybody who'd ever been a member, no matter how young they were or how short their association. The slightest step out of line spelled doom."

[25]Id, p. 133. Red Channels named 151 actors and other artists with alleged ties to communism—from musician Pete Seeger to movie star Edward G. Robinson—who it said should be hired…

Though the FBI had removed ABL eight years earlier, they had kept tabs on him. A memo to Tolson dated July 18, 1947, from a J. P. Mohr entitled "[Redacted], FORMER SPECIAL AGENT, HUAC," reads in part: "[Redacted] came in to see me this afternoon and stated that he had accepted the position to head the investigation of communist infiltration in the movie industry in Hooywood (misspelled in the original). He stated he is to receive $25 per day and that they also hired his associate, A.B. Leckie, and he is to receive $22.50 per day. The committee informed him that he could hire as many investigators and clerical employees as he needed to conduct the investigation properly.

"[Redacted] states the objective of his investigation is to go out there between now and September 27, 1947, which has been set as the tentative sate (misspelling in original) for hearings in Washington, DC, to line up friendly witnesses can (misspelling in original) those unfriendly witnesses which the committee will desire to call. He said his purpose in that connection would be to line up about twenty-five to thirty good witnesses who can, through proper questioning, expose the entire communist infiltration of the movie industry.

"[Redacted] said that he had a long discussion this morning with [Lengthy Redaction], who outlined the history of the Dies Committee and particularly its efforts to investigate communist infiltration in the movie industry. [Redacted] told him a man by the name of [Redacted] was sent out to Hollywood tin (misspelling in original) 1938 and 1939, that [Redacted] made his investigation and apparently while on board the train back to Washington, DC, he got drunk and exposed the entire investigation. He said [Redacted] was characterized as being a drunkard, and after writing his report, which apparently was ineffectual, he was dis-[Redacted]."

ABL may have been down, but in the mind of Hoover, he most certainly was not out.

Hearings by the HUAC started in 1947, but the committee itself began back in 1934. ABL was—once again—right in the thick of things. Once my father finally started talking about his father in the 1990s, my dad loved telling me new stories, including details of how his dad brought him to carry out surveillance and plant bugs in the homes of alleged left-wing sympathetic actors and actresses. He would relate stories that seemed to be straight out of the movies.

One of them went like this:

"Bunny, get up. It's time to go."

"OK, Dad. I'm ready".

They would get into ABL's new Buick and drive through the Hollywood Hills, Brentwood, Bel-Air, and other ritzy parts of town where the film stars, directors, and producers lived. They had to drive into the less glamorous parts of town to invade the privacy of the writers, who then, as now, always got the short end of the pay stick.

"We would park somewhere near the house we were targeting, and when we were sure no one was home, we would find a way to get in and plant bugs. My dad usually preferred lamp shades, but sometimes we would put them onto the underside of tables and under mattresses," my dad explained. Other times, they would rifle through people's mail, take down car license plate numbers, and simply watch the comings and goings of visitors to whichever person they were focused on at any given time. I shudder to think how these antics ruined so many lives.

While much of this work was highly secretive, a solid chunk of it was very public. A newspaper article from July 21, 1947, by the International News Service, reads as follows: "Representative Thomas, republican of New Jersey and chairman of the HUAC, today appointed two former FBI agents to make on-the-spot investigations of communism in Hollywood. Thomas named H. A. Smith as chief of the West Coast investigative staff and A.B. Leckie as his assistant. Both are residents of Los Angeles. Smith, a graduate of the USC, served as a special agent for the FBI for seven years, supervising investigations regarding subversive activities in national defense. Leckie was a special FBI agent for five years. Thomas announced that the appointment of the two investigators was "for the purpose of intensifying the investigation, which is to result in public hearings in Washington in September."

The hearings were, indeed, held two months later, spanning a total of 188 hours. In photographs from the crowded chamber, ABL sat just meters away from Richard M. Nixon during testimony by Jack L. Warner of Warner Bros. fame, testifying about "alleged communist activities in Hollywood." In another newspaper photograph, ABL marched hand-in-hand in front of the US Capital dome with famous actor Robert Taylor "surrounded by a crowd of enthusiastic women" after testifying before the HUAC. The caption reads, "Hundreds of women formed a Pied-Piper-like procession behind him for more than a block."

An article in *Time Magazine* in November 1947 discussed the intrusive work of the HUAC: "Next day, as all Washington knew, Robert Taylor would appear. The crowds were even bigger and earlier. Handsome actor Taylor had a point to clear up. When Chairman Thomas had sleuthed out to Hollywood last summer for a preliminary sniff, Taylor had announced that he had been forced by New Deal pressure to appear in MGM's 'Song of Russia.' Said he now, 'I wasn't forced because they can't force you to take any picture.' But he was sure that communist pressures were rising in Hollywood, and he offered the same cure-all ... 'If I had my way about it, they'd all be sent back to Russia or some other unpleasant place.' He was a success: when he had finished, more than half the spectators stamped for the door, clustered happily around him, and followed him triumphantly more than a block down the street to his automobile."[26]

Another series of pictures during the McCarthy hearings held in 1947 shows ABL sitting adjacent to the future scandal-ridden President Richard Nixon who, of course, arrived on the national political scene as a result of his key role in the McCarthy trials. These hearings were not harmless public outings of alleged leftish sympathizers but rather destroyed countless careers in the entertainment industry.[27]

Having been brought up in a conservative Republican family, as a child, my proud Nixon-voting parents would often take me to Nixon's

---

[26]National Affairs: The Congress "Hollywood on the Hill," *Time*, November 3, 1947.

[27]"Of considerable concern to the committee was the entertainment industry with its tremendous capacity to instruct and influence and, deserved or not, the careers of many talented men and women were destroyed. Some suffered what might be called professional death; others absolutely committed suicide. Those who survived were glad to eke out a living by performing menial tasks." Source: Matthew Smith, *The Men Who Murdered Marilyn*, Bloomsbury, 1996, p. 125.

favorite restaurant near his San Clemente home, referred to as the Western White House. I was giddy with joy every time I was allowed to sit in Nixon's chair at El Adobe, a huge, oversized chair with a little golden plaque on the back that said something like "Richard M. Nixon's Favorite Chair." I couldn't believe my luck, having no idea yet about the illegal bombing of Cambodia, his countless dirty tricks, and most certainly Watergate, nor did I realize that several of Nixon's closest advisors, including some eventually convicted and imprisoned because of their roles in the Watergate scandal, lived in my neighborhood, including one who lived just three houses away down my street.

Newspaper accounts after the hearings noted that, "Bernard Leckie was in Greenville for the weekend, *en route* to his home in Los Angeles, from Washington, where he testified before the Congressional Investigation Committee regarding communist activities in the movie industry. Mr. Leckie accompanied a group of movie stars to Washington. When he was testifying, he was asked where he was born. He said that he answered loudly and proudly: 'Greenville, Alabama.'"

The official publication of the Society of Former Special Agents of the FBI, *The Grapevine*, reported on ABL's appointment to head what became known as the Hollywood purges, noting that, "Together with Congressman H. Allan Smith, he was appointed by the HUAC to investigate communism in the motion picture industry and later testified at hearings in Washington."

My grandfather's picture appears next to actor Cary Grant during his testimony to the (HUAC) during the hearings held on October 23, 1947. According to Goldstein, and in reference to the trials, "in their wake, careers were ruined, friendships were lost, and studio films were changed forever ... the hearings sparked a campaign of anti-communist hysteria that swept through Hollywood, then the State Department, labor unions, academia, and the armed forces."[28] These long-forgotten days seem to have returned to the US today.

ABL was involved in exposing alleged communists in Hollywood for years. An index card-sized invitation to a 1949 event hosted by the Beverly Hills Alumni Association of SAE read, "Presents for your entertainment—Don't Miss This Program. "Inside of Crime and the Undercover of Communistic Activity in America" by A.B. Leckie undercover investigator—eight years with the FBI—four years security intelligence US Navy—two years exposing the reds in Hollywood for the Thomas Committee. What a story he has to tell! Tuesday—February 22. 6:30 p.m. at Eaton's, 8500 Burton Way, LA. Bring a brother with you."

Articles and books abound about the infamous Hollywood purges. One entitled *Hollywood Red Probe Ultimatum: Smith Gives Film City 60 Days to Oust Subversives*. It was Smith, of course, the former FBI agent who worked together hand-in-hand with ABL during these dark days in support of the nefarious aims of the HUAC. As evidence of just how wrong this whole enterprise was, Louis B. Mayer, the head of MGM at the time, and after whom part of its name derived, fired a writer working for the studio named Lester Cole, a suspected communist supporter. Smith and ABL had told Mayer that Cole was behind the communist messages in the film *Song of Russia*, which they deemed communist propaganda. Mayer replied that there was no

---

[28]See, for instance: James Adams and Maurice Chittenden, Hoover of the FBI had stars in his eyes, *The Sunday Times*, 2 February 1997 and Patrick Goldstein, The Birth of the Blacklist, *LA Times*, October 19, 1997. "HUAC began its hearings on Oct 20, 1947, with its rotund committee chairman, J. Parnell Thomas ... two future presidents were on hand, Richard Nixon as a member of the HUAC, and Ronald Reagan as a friendly witness. Nineteen unfriendly witnesses were subpoenaed, mostly suspected communist writers and directors. Ten eventually testified, refusing to discuss their party affiliations or name party members. Known as the Hollywood 10, they were found in contempt of Congress, fired from their jobs, and eventually sent to prison." "Actors who flew to Washington to object to hearings included June Havoc, Danny Kaye, Marsha Hunt, Humphrey Bogart, Lauren Becall, Evelyn Keyes, and Paul Henreid." "Eventually hundreds of film and TV writers, directors, and actors suffered the same fate, forced to leave the country or work under false names."

communism in the picture and that they couldn't substantiate the charge. Nevertheless, Cole was fired because he refused to testify before the HUAC.

Interestingly, as far as ABL goes, despite their ideological similarities, Hoover's ego did not allow him to like Senator McCarthy very much: "McCarthy has supplanted the FBI director as the nation's chief enemy of communism", said one analysis.[29] A lifelong feud between these two communist haters ensued as both vied for attention based on who was more anti-communist than the other.

Sexual orientation may have tied these men together as well. It was not just Hoover and Tolson who successfully sought, during their lifetimes at least, to hide their homosexuality, but so, too, did Joseph McCarthy, who was also thought to have been secretly gay.[30] Moreover, Roy Cohn, one of McCarthy's most well-known lawyers, whose secretly gay life was recently explored in detail in a 2019 film, reveals the harsh reality that being gay in the 1950s was particularly challenging for those in public life. Typically, people took every possible measure to hide one's sexual orientation.[31] Could it really be true that the head of the FBI, his deputy, the head of the (HUAC), and its principal lawyer were all secretly gay, all the while hounding other gay people and destroying their lives because they loved the wrong sex? To what degree did their secrets lead to a particularly virulent strain of homophobic repression as yet another tool of attempting to hide a truth that would have been life- and career-destroying in 1950s America? Is it merely coincidence that these powerful—and possibly gay men—hired ABL, or is this a new side of my grandfather not many others seem to have ever known about? I don't know, but I wonder.

Around this time, at the end of his communist-hunting years, some

---

[29]Cartha D. "Deke" DeLoach, *Hoover's FBI: The Inside Story by Hoover's Trusted Lieutenant*, Regnery Publishing Inc., 1995, p. 352.

[30]Deloach notes that McCarthy was accused of "sex crimes, including homosexual acts ... with dates of gay sex parties ... Then Senator William B. Benton of Connecticut received a letter, laced with obscenities, that accused McCarthy of sodomizing several American servicemen." *Id.*, p. 352.

[31]On the Cohn film, see the film *Where's My Roy Cohn?* (2019).

funny friends of ABL arranged for a mock-up of the *Hollywood Journal* newspaper. It shows a fake—and massive—headline in huge capital letters: "X-RAY OF LECKIE'S HEAD SHOWS NOTHING."

In September 1949, the California Detective License Bureau registered ABL as an investigator after two busy years of hunting communists. This work led to some strange experiences in subsequent years. In fact, I believe these may have killed him, even though his diabetes, diagnosed the following year, was officially listed as his cause of death.

Chapter 8

Bunny's Booth

A full decade after leaving the FBI, ABL continued to communicate with Hoover, and in 1949, he received a letter from him, thanking ABL for his congratulations on his twenty-fifth anniversary at the FBI. Two weeks before the 1952 presidential election, ABL received a letter from the Republican National Committee, taking delight in learning that he was "standing so strongly with us in the effort we are making to place Ike Eisenhower at the helm of our country in the critical years which lie ahead—with the immediate result of removing from our country the heavy yoke of that political monstrosity known as the New Deal—Fair Deal." A newspaper article also from 1952 noted that A.B. Leckie was "a plump sleuth who used to be an FBI man."

One intriguing physical aspect of ABL's legacy was the hundreds of postcards he wrote, kept by their recipients and assembled into small brown boxes. I knew of these cards but never felt compelled to read them until it became time for me to write his story. Once I discovered these, I read them not once, not twice, but countless times. With each reading, I discovered just a little bit more, a small sliver of something I had missed before, and that helped me understand other materials, allowing an ever more real picture of ABL's life to emerge.

These cards tell me quite a bit about ABL. In fact—aside from the contents of the cards—just holding them in my hands almost a century after he did (presumably with at least traces of his DNA still upon their surfaces, though the exquisite double-helix of the DNA molecule itself was still yet to be discovered when they were written)—sends shivers down my spine. They intensify as I delve deeper into deciphering where he was when he scribbled his gentle but messy words and who last sharpened the pencil that transferred his thoughts from his Leckie brain onto the fraying paper that were once mighty trees. Who thought up the ideas of what image to capture and place onto these cards? Who wrote the captions? Some are so old that the images they capture are hand-painted photos of places like orange groves, Hollenbeck Park in LA, or the famous Ambassador Hotel, a place that figured prominently in both ABL's life—as well as the country as a whole.

Around this time, ABL's dedication to the Tail o' the Cock began, legendary and unrivaled. But his propensity for bars, ballrooms, and tackily decorated conference rooms also led him to frequently visit the famous Ambassador Hotel. This huge and imposing hotel covered twenty-two acres of prime LA real estate and, among other things, hosted what was called the world-famous Cocoanut Grove. One of ABL's postcards showed the inside of the Cocoanut Grove, replete with life-sized fake palm trees (it wouldn't be LA without them) and scores of round tables covered in white table clothes arranged in a semi-circle in front of a bandstand—each table completed by those institutional chairs so common to the US, in horrible shades of alternating orange and green. I'm not sure if this was the precise location where Bobby Kennedy gave his final speech before exiting the Embassy Ballroom on June 5, 1968, before being shot down in the kitchen area of this famous landmark, but it certainly could be.

The caption of one card describes the hotel in the following way: "An exciting, fabulous hotel with twenty-two acres of resort facilities located in the heart of the city. Everything imaginable for comfort, pleasure, or business. Home of the renowned Cocoanut Grove." The other card depicting this renowned establishment said, "One of the world's most fabulous supper clubs, the COCOANUT GROVE. Here, every night is filled with glamour and romance as you mingle with Hollywood's most famous stage and international personalities. The food and service are superb, the entertainment offers show [the] world's brightest stars plus music by the nation's top orchestras."

Of all the letters exchanged between ABL and Hoover, none were provided by the FBI under my FOIA requests. ABL must have kept copies of these letters, with one directly mentioning the Ambassador Hotel by name; it is perhaps the most compelling. This historical merger of people, places, time, and history, where ABL meshed and merged with Hoover, Bobby Kennedy, Sirhan Sirhan, and so many others, captures so much of the essence of LA in the 1960s. Glamour and tragedy entwined as the hope of Kennedy's Camelot, along with the 1960s themselves, came to a sad and screeching halt.

ABL did not write all of the cards. He received several at various LA addresses, including his favorite bar. Another, sent on July 10, 1957, from the Pike's Peak area of Colorado, went to his private eye's office on Wilshire from someone called Roscoe. In it, he tantalizingly wrote, "There's a lot of natural beauty around here. Wait until I tell you about her." Oddly, there is also another postcard dating back to June 17, 1925, written to ABL's parents in Alabama, almost as if playing the role of an ancient Greek scribe.

The card reads, "Dear Mrs. Leckie, I am a very good friend of your Bernard. He is working on a ranch in the town (Owensmouth, CA) where I live. I got him the job. He seems to like it. Bernard told me to write you, as he had no stationary but that he would get some soon. Love to all." I don't know about you, but the film *Brokeback Mountain* just crossed my mind.

At this time in his life—and for years—the daily venue remained the same. Day in, day out—same booth, same bottle, same decor, same result. Only his food choices changed, and even those simply alternated between the roast tom turkey for $2.75 and the grilled, thick eastern pork chops (with apple sauce) for a slightly less affordable $2.85, and on nights he wanted to splurge, he went with the famous charcoal broiled Tail o' the Cock pepper steak, which set him back a daunting $4.50. Mac McHenry's Tail o' the Cock, the go-to dinner spot for so many of Hollywood's finest, started up in 1939 and soon thereafter became the official/unofficial place of business for ABL from the late 1940s until his untimely demise in 1962. With a logo proudly proclaiming The Cock to be a one-of-a-kind restaurant, little wonder this watering hole was the place of so many Tinsel Town deals over the years.

It's hard to say just how much The Cock's daily routine influenced ABL's weakness for the bottle, but during this time, something increasingly serious must have gotten to him. Whatever scale of alcoholism he suffered from in his early years, it worsened considerably in the 1950s and early 1960s. At first, he would arrive early and sit straight up, back firm, as if in a church pew, while he ordered his first drink of the day. Yet, as every night wore on, he would slide further and further down the red leather booth seats at his corner table as the empty part of the bottle began to dominate whatever amber fluid remained. Legend has it that he regularly drank at least a full bottle of whisky there every night, holding court to all who wished to listen, Early Times being his favorite. Almost as frequent as his nightly visits, McHenry often had no choice but to call my father, even during his high school days at Fairfax High. My father would come down at closing time to peel his inebriated father from his chair and get him safely home. These memories must have influenced my dad's lifelong moderation with alcohol and probably formed at least part of his reluctance to ever mention ABL.

It took a full thirty years to get past those Early Times before my dad was comfortable enough to spill some pretty interesting beans about his sometimes-troublesome pop, pickled liver and all. It remains unclear whether the Tail o' the Cock could have been a code name for another type of establishment. Men with perfect bodies were certainly far from absent from this famous haunt. According to some who frequented the joint, one of the bouncers at the Tail o' the Cock was an actor known for shirtless roles in Hollywood, who even played Tarzan in the movies.

As might be imagined, the Tail o' the Cock exuded an unmistakable aroma that all who entered noticed, with the sole exception of people like ABL, who spent so much time there that they barely noticed it anymore. No one who came in for the first time could miss it, however, as much as they may have wished to. Stale alcohol infused with cigarette smoke, overused cooking oil, and the remnants of barbequed meat—both recent and ancient—created an atmosphere attractive to those who loved it and repulsive to those who didn't. The Cock, as regulars called it, was decorated with a woodsy feel, much like a rustic cabin high in the mountains. It was replete with portions of full tree trunks still covered with bark, wooden beams, a large stone fireplace, an indoor garden, and tables with white tablecloths. A postcard from this era extols the greatness of this Hollywood hot spot in the following way: "Located in the heart of famous Restaurant Row, the Tail o' the Cock is famed for its unsurpassed cuisine and friendly, courteous service. A gracious, homelike atmosphere and beautiful surroundings have established it as one of the West's most popular restaurants." It was certainly so for my grandfather.

Located at 477 S. La Cienega Blvd in LA, what was once the Tail o' the Cock suffered the fate Joni Mitchell warned us about all those years ago and now exists as one of the thousands of space-wasting parking lots on a busy and famous LA road. In its heyday, though, The Cock was an immensely popular dinner place famous for its American menus and bar scene. According to one account, "The Tail o' the Cock claimed to be the first place in Los Angeles to serve margaritas ... As one might gather from the name, the big selling point at the Tail o' the Cock wasn't the food so much as the cocktails. It was a popular place for people to meet for drinks, especially late in the afternoon. People consummated an awful lot of Hollywood deals over their martinis. It was where a voice actress name June Foray met with two animation producers—Jay Ward and Bill Scott. They told her they wanted her to play a new character named Rocky the Flying Squirrel. Undoubtedly, there were less important roles cast in these booths, some involving big Academy Award productions."[32]

You could find plenty of Hollywood vibes in the area during those days. For those who had had enough of The Cock for the night, they could walk not all far down the road for the salty seadog feel and visit Alan's Hale's Lobster Barrel, owned by the blue-shirted captain of the

---

[32]www.povonline.com/larestaurants/larestaurants06.com.

well-known TV series *Gilligan's Island*.

As the years wore on, ABL spent an ever-greater portion of every day at the Tail o' the Cock. In all likelihood, sometimes people who shouldn't have been listening would purposely sit just a table or two away, carefully eavesdropping on the famous eavesdropper himself. And all too often, he probably didn't even notice. One late afternoon in 1959, Bunny began the daily quest for inebriation when Mac stopped by his table with a postcard addressed to ABL at The Cock, not his home or Wilshire Blvd office but to the renowned home of the margarita.

In handing over the postcard, Mac could have said: "Hey, Bunny, I got another postcard for ya. I think it's from England," as he handed over the hand-written card with serrated edges and a rather surreal old photo of French fishmongers standing proudly with overflowing baskets of fresh oysters, lobsters, mussels, and lemons. Passersby would have found it hard to resist the display. Three men in the picture stood outside their romantic stall, one dressed in yellow plaid with a belly at least as large as Bunny's and the other two standing side by side, dressed in royal blue tops, starring rather seductively down the camera lens. The photo was clearly taken in France or at least in a French-speaking area. But oddly, the card was postmarked to South Kensington SW1 and covered in four brown two pence postage stamps picturing a very young Queen Elisabeth II.

"Thanks, Mac," said Bunny. "I wonder who it's from?" Once he adjusted to the limited light in the darkened corner of the restaurant, he looked first not at the picture, not at the stamps, not at the postmark, but at the very bottom of the card, where it was written for all the world to see, "Love and kisses, Johnny."

Atop the card, Bunny's friend Johnny had written, "Please turn over," underlining it for effect, thus urging ABL to glance at the picture of the fishermen before reading. And what followed was this: "Hi! I can't help thinking this is where you got your start. They all seem to know you, but now then, all are band leaders." It ends there with the salutation expressing *love and kisses*.

Even comparatively progressive Hollywood and LA were deeply homophobic during the 1950s. Any inkling that one was gay could sink a career and even a life; it was remarkable that good ole Johnny so publicly wrote such words to Bunny. Anyone could have read them. Being gay—or even being suspected of being so—in much of the US at the time was not just scandalous. It was criminal in some jurisdictions. Tragically and shamefully, being gay is still outlawed in more than sixty countries, and, in some, the penalty is death. It was not something anyone, let alone someone involved in espionage and law enforcement, would want to be associated with them. But it didn't seem to bother either Johnny or Bunny too much. Johnny's name ended up in ABL's private address book, with hearts and asterisks nearby.

As he finished reading the card for probably the fourth time, he remembered an upcoming appointment with officials from Trans World Airlines. No sooner had he recalled this appointment than two employees from America's first great airline company approached his table. They must have both had pleasant, but stern looks on their faces, and recognizing ABL, they spoke.

"Mr. Leckie, I'm Mr. Hayes, and this is Mr. Olson from TWA. I'm so glad you could meet us here today."

"Well, my pleasure, gentlemen, can I offer you a drink? They invented a thing called the margarita here in case you're interested."

They looked down at his bottle of Early Times and gladly accepted the offer of a drink in a salt-lined glass. "Anything is better than Early Times," they silently said to each other with their eyes.

"Mac! Two margaritas for these fine, upstanding gents, please."

"Speaking of gents," Hayes said. "Please excuse me for a moment," and off he went to find the men's room. He was unable to find it immediately, tucked away as it was far from the prying eyes of either customers or hopeful stargazers. He noticed a chef on a break leaning on a wall just out of an eyeshot of the crowded dining room.

Looking down at the cook's apron, he saw the man's name and asked, "Excuse me, Ron, can you please let me know where I can find the facilities?" Ron just raised his right arm and pointed to a small door in the corner. Then off he went.

Just a few weeks prior, Marlon Brando, another long-time client of ABL, had asked Ron the very same question. It left Ron to wonder if there was something about him that made people think he knew where it was. Hayes quickly returned to the table, possibly noticing along the way two men equally out of place, dressed far too formally and far too uncomfortably for The Cock. He watched them from the corner of his eye, staring right back at him and the goings-on at Bunny's booth.

"Welcome back," said Bunny. "Everything come out OK?" It was an old and typically tactless joke, and yet, he chuckled, expecting a laugh in return but receiving only looks of bemusement. The arrival of the drinks broke the ice again, and they all held up their drinks for a three-way cheers.

"So, shall we get down to business?" said Hayes.

"Sure thing," replied Bunny.

"I suppose you know why we're here, Mr. Leckie?"

"I can guess."

"Well, that's right. As everyone knows, you were the first and only private eye to find Howard Hughes when he first went into hiding, and, well, we need to find him one more time. He's disappeared yet again, and we need to serve him with papers regarding a pending TWA case. Unless we find him, no papers will be served and no case. Can you help us? Can you try to find him again and deliver these papers?"

Without the slightest hesitation, Bunny smiled the pudgy smile of contentment he got when a new contract landed unexpectedly in his lap and simply said, "You bet I can."

Though his regular inebriation at the Tail o' the Cock surely must have dented his body and reputation, on the work front, he was still very much on top of his game. Based purely on his FBI experiences and track record, an agency hired him to trace Howard Hughes twice. He succeeded both times. He found him first hiding in Las Vegas after Hughes pulled what was called "the most successful vanishing act since Houdini." Allegedly, ABL was the only private investigator to find Hughes during his disappearance. In the hugely popular *Saturday Evening Post* of February 9, 1963, published half a year after his death, a subsection of an article entitled "A Platoon-sized Manhunt" reads as follows: "Beginning a little over a year ago, an intense effort to locate Hughes was launched by a platoon of skilled private investigators, hired by Wall Street, management of TWA, in order to serve the elusive multimillionaire with legal papers in their battle for the airline. This private manhunt was headed by a shrewd little sleuth named A.B. Leckie, who had unique qualifications for the job. Leckie was the only private investigator ever known to have found Hughes, having traced him years before to a resort hotel in Las Vegas at the behest of a suspicious movie actress whom Hughes had been squiring around. In the TWA manhunt, a bizarre secret war was soon raging between Leckie's legion and Hughes's own security forces, commanded by a former FBI agent. Frustrated at every turn, Leckie finally staked out the residence of Hughes's top troubleshooter. The Hughes field general spotted the opposition's field general, sallied forth, and gently chided him for playing cloak-and-dagger with another professional." The field general of which they speak was, in fact, having been a trainee of ABLs at Quantico years before, at a distinct disadvantage, and ABL certainly won this battle.

The rather gloomy red cover of *The Post* that February in 1963 featured a story touted as, "From behind the Iron Curtain: The Anti-Stalin Novel that Rocked the Communist World," while ABL's article was extolled as "Missing Millionaire: The Truth About Howard Hughes." It's as if Elon Musk or Jeff Bezos repeatedly hid themselves away for months or years in a secret lair, their whereabouts unknown, only to be found by a shrewd sleuth named Leckie. Incredible.

By then, having worked the streets of LA for decades and knowing just about everyone who was anyone, within a few days, ABL found the world's richest man for the second time. He successfully served him with the legal papers on the TWA case, and then, it was all in the hands of the lawyers.

To celebrate another job done and dusted, Bunny probably went back to Tail o' the Cock that night and re-enacted what he did every night before for the previous decade or two: ordered his Early Times and got right into it. Three-quarters of the way through the bottle, he may have scanned the room for the umpteenth time that night. Perhaps this night was just a touch different than so many others. I can imagine him looking around, of course, recognizing everyone except for two men sitting just three tables away. At first, he would have thought they were newcomers to The Cock, but looking closer, it might have suddenly dawned on him that it was the same two guys who were staring at him when the TWA duo arrived a few days prior. He rumpled his eyebrows, being careful not to let them see his discomfort, then called Mac over to the table. He positioned himself so that Mac would have his back to the two irregulars, keeping both of them hidden,

Bunny, who trusted Mac implicitly, may have whispered, "Who are those two guys at Table Twenty-Seven? I saw them here a few days ago, and now they're here again, staring at me intensely." Mac casually looked around, as if looking toward the bar, noticed who ABL was talking about, and might have replied, "Some guys from the Washington, I think. Maybe intelligence or something; I'm not sure. I think that actor guy was talking to them the other night."

"Holy shit," muttered Bunny under his breath. "Please tell me you didn't tell them about Marilyn."

"After that rant you went on the other night, embarrassing yourself and everyone around you, saying this and that about how close you are to Marilyn and how you discovered who was spying on her. Believe me, Bunny, your relations with Marilyn are anything but a secret to anyone at The Cock," Mac said ominously.

Photographs of ABL

**Hand-drawn poster of ABL sitting and Hoover looming
large over him with a memorable quote.
Why did Hoover then ruthlessly fire him just months later?**

ABL in his high school years.

Dapper college student.

A young ABL.

ABL on one of his many cross country road trips.

A young ABL at the beach making a universal gesture.

ABL's first wedding day.

A contemplative crime solver at work.

To A. B. Leckie with cordial regards from your friend,
11/2/35 J. Edgar Hoover.

The proud G-man at his desk with Hoover photo looming large in the background.

My father declining an offer to join the FBI at age 6.

ABL during his first weeks as a G-man.

The new G-man realizing the job he had just agreed to do.

Newspaper report on ABL's arrival in Philadelphia.

Federal Bureau of Investigation
United States Department of Justice
Washington, D. C.

August 22, 1939

Mr. A. Bernard Leckie
Federal Bureau of Investigation
United States Department of Justice
607 United States Court House, Foley Square
New York, New York

Dear Mr. Leckie:

I have your very kind letter of August 18, 1939, with reference to your resignation as a Special Agent in the Federal Bureau of Investigation and I want to thank you for explaining why you have taken this action. You are entering a most worthy field of endeavor, and I hope that the experience gained with this organization will be of benefit to you. I am sure that you will meet with marked success in your new work, and if I can be of any assistance please do not hesitate to call upon me.

In accordance with your request your resignation is being accepted effective at the close of business November 23, 1939, active duty to cease at the close of business August 24th.

With kindest regards,

Sincerely yours,

J. Edgar Hoover

Surely the worst letter ABL ever received.

Testimonial Dinner in honor of ABL - the night be received the hand-drawn cartoon of him and Hoover.

ABL mxing it up with local police.

PENN ATHLETIC CLUB

VOL. 9   No. 11   *Forecast*   MARCH 12, 1938

PHILADELPHIA'S TOP G-MAN

MR. A. B. LECKIE

*Special Agent in Charge of the Philadelphia Office of the Federal Bureau of Investigation
of the United States Department of Justice*

MEN'S WEEKLY LUNCHEON

THURSDAY, MARCH 17th   BALLROOM   12.30 P. M. $1.00

Subject: "THE PUBLIC AND LAW ENFORCEMENT"

The title gives you no idea of the thrills in store for you when this ace tracker of America's most desperate criminals tells of his experiences throughout the country in the line of duty. He has had four years of it and has participated in all the famous major cases solved by the indomitable members of this most famous body of man-hunters in the world.

For a year he was the right-hand man of J. Edgar Hoover, as he was the Administrative Assistant to the Director of the Federal Bureau of Investigation in Washington. He knows all the answers to all your questions as to how this organization of intrepid men—the most feared by criminals and the most admired by the law-abiding—always "Gets Its Man."

When you hear this talk, you'll get all the thrills of a G-Man's life without subjecting yourself to any of its hazards.

Also plan to come to the Luncheon on Thursday, March 24th. The Weekly Luncheon Committee has arranged for a Great Stage Show.

ABL - Philadephia's Top G-Man!

Federal Bureau of Investigation

United States Department of Justice

Washington, D. C.

June 3, 1939

Mr. A. B. Leckie
Federal Bureau of Investigation
U. S. Department of Justice
1300 Liberty Trust Building
Philadelphia, Pennsylvania

Dear Mr. Leckie:

You are hereby directed to proceed to Chicago, Illinois, via Washington, D. C., public business permitting, and assume the duties of Special Agent in Charge of the Chicago Field Division.

Very truly yours,

John Edgar Hoover
Director

What may appear a promotion was, in fact, the beginning of the end.

Federal Bureau of Investigation
United States Department of Justice
Washington, D. C.

July 5, 1938

Mr. A. B. Leckie
Federal Bureau of Investigation
U. S. Department of Justice
1300 Liberty Trust Building
Philadelphia, Pennsylvania

Dear Mr. Leckie:-

The records of the Bureau show that the average regular overtime service performed by you per working day during the period from February to May, 1938, inclusive, was 5 hours and 45 minutes.

While I appreciate your industry, I do feel that this is an excessive amount of overtime and I desire that you endeavor to reduce the number of overtime hours of work which you perform. Although it is realized that there will always be overtime on the part of Bureau representatives and while I am anxious to have this overtime performed on an equitable basis by field employees, I do not feel that any employee should continue in his work to such an extent that it may impair his physical health. I hope that it will be possible for you to reduce the amount of time which you have been spending on official duties.

With kind regards,

Sincerely,

J. Edgar Hoover

Critical letter from Hoover to ABL admonishing him for
working too much.

ABL in his Navy outfit standing next to Clyde Tolson (on his right), the man most likely to have been responsible for his unceremonious departure from his beloved FBI.

JOHN EDGAR HOOVER
DIRECTOR

Federal Bureau of Investigation
United States Department of Justice
Washington, D. C.

October 11, 1937.

Mr. A. B. Leckie,
Federal Bureau of Investigation,
U. S. Department of Justice,
Washington, D. C.

Dear Mr. Leckie:

I wish to take this opportunity of expressing my appreciation for the efficient manner in which you discharged your assignments as a member of the Entertainment Committee during the recent 23rd Annual Convention of the International Association for Identification. On many occasions, I personally observed the manner in which you were greeting the various delegates and I do want you to know that I appreciate your untiring efforts in this respect.

With best wishes and kind regards,

Sincerely yours,

J. Edgar Hoover

Friendly letter from Hoover to ABL.

JOHN EDGAR HOOVER
DIRECTOR

Federal Bureau of Investigation
United States Department of Justice
Washington, D. C.

January 5, 1938.

Dear Mr. Leckie:

        It was indeed thoughtful of you
to send me the fine telegram of Birthday
and New Year Greetings and I want you to
know how deeply appreciative I am of your
so remembering me.

                    Sincerely,

                    J. Edgar Hoover

Mr. A. B. Leckie,
The Lafayette Hotel,
Washington, D. C.

Another personal note to ABL from Hoover.

As a member of the International Secretariat of the

United Nations Conference
on
International Organization

San Francisco 1945

A.B. Leckie

has, by faithful and diligent performance of duty, contributed to the creation of the Charter of the United Nations. This certificate is awarded in grateful acknowledgment.

E. Stettinius Jr.

Alger Hiss

Certificate issued to ABL for his work at the conference establishing the United Nations in 1945. Note signature by Alger Hiss who was later accused of spying for the Soviet Union.

PROGRAM

Closing Plenary Session • The United Nations Conference on International Organization • San Francisco, June 26, 1945

Rare original booklet issued on the final day of the UN Conference on June 26, 1945.

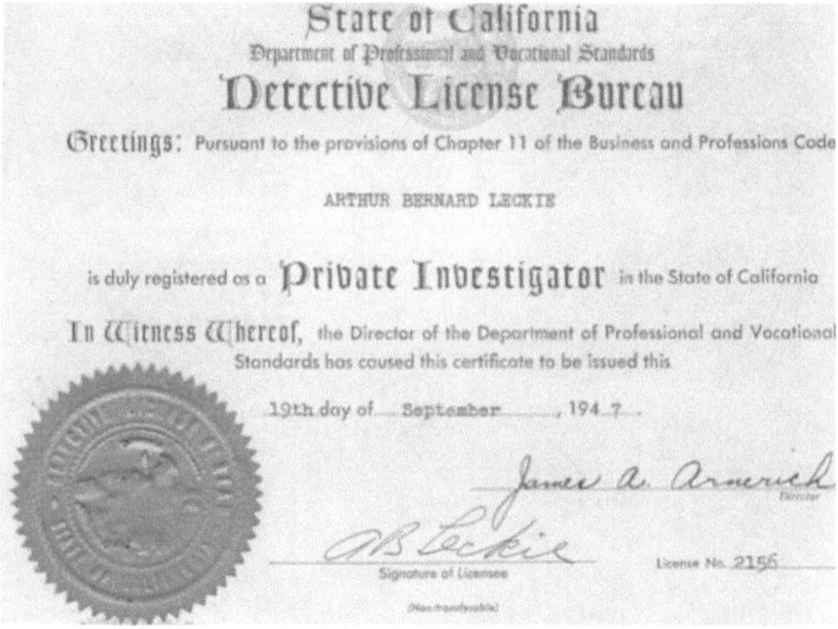

State of California
Department of Professional and Vocational Standards
Detective License Bureau

Greetings: Pursuant to the provisions of Chapter 11 of the Business and Professions Code

ARTHUR BERNARD LECKIE

is duly registered as a Private Investigator in the State of California

In Witness Whereof, the Director of the Department of Professional and Vocational Standards has caused this certificate to be issued this

19th day of September, 1947.

James A. Arnerich
Director

A B Leckie
Signature of Licensee

License No. 2156

(Non-transferable)

ABL becomes a private eye.

Federal Bureau of Investigation
United States Department of Justice
Washington 25, D. C.

May 11, 1949

Mr. A. Bernard Leckie
449 North Orlando Avenue
Los Angeles, California

Dear Mr. Leckie:

I have your wire of congratulations, and wanted to take this means to thank you for your thoughtfulness in taking time to remember me on my Twenty-fifth Anniversary.

It is a source of deep encouragement to realize that although you are no longer associated with the Bureau its progress has been followed by you with such great interest.

With best wishes,

Sincerely,

J. Edgar Hoover

A full ten years after leaving the FBI, ABL received this from his once close friend, J. Edgar Hoover.

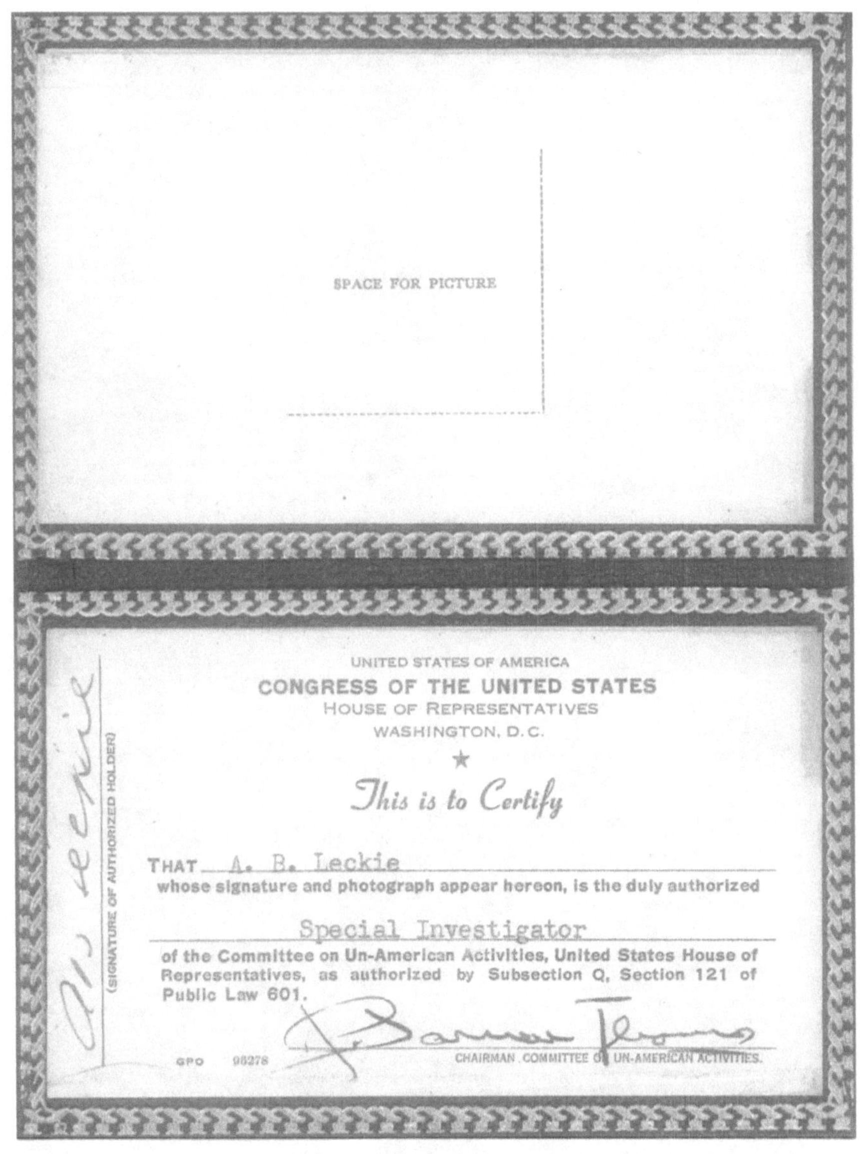

ABL's ID card for his work with the US House Committee
on Un-American Activities.

ABL with heartthrob actor Robert Taylor during the McCarthy Trials.

ABL and Robert Taylor march down the street after ABL'as orchestrated testimony by movie star Robert Taylor

By International News Service.

WASHINGTON, July 21 — Representative Thomas, Republican of New Jersey, chairman of the House Un-American Activities Committee, today appointed two former FBI agents to make special investigations of Communism in Hollywood.

Thomas named H. A. Smith as chief of the West Coast investigative staff and A. B. Leckie as his assistant. Both are residents of Los Angeles.

Smith, a graduate of the University of Southern California, served as a special agent for the FBI for seven years, supervising investigation regarding subversive activities in national defense.

Leckie was a special FBI agent for five years.

Thomas announced that the appointment of the two investigators was "for the purpose of intensifying the investigation which is to result in public hearings in Washington in September."

ABL at the far right side of the image looking back into the chamber during one of the controversial hearings of the House Committee on Un-American Activities, chaired during this meeting by future US.

ABL and his private eye mobile, white-walled tires and all the rest.

Interior shot of ABL's daily haunt, the Tail o' the Cock on
La Cienega in LA. Oh, if those walls could talk.

McHENRY'S
Tail o' the Cock

477 S. La Cienega Blvd.   Los Angeles 48
CRestview 5-5173

Located in the heart of famous Restaurant
Row, the Tail o' the Cock is famed for its
unsurpassed cuisine and friendly, courteous
service. Gracious homelike atmosphere and
beautiful surroundings have established it as
one of the West's most popular restaurants.
Open from 11:30 A.M. daily.

Card by TriColor Multiprint Corp., Hollywood 27. Calif. · Carl Junghans Photo

POST CARD

PLACE
3 CENT
STAMP
HERE

Back side of the postcard issued by Mac McHenry, owner of the Tail o' the Cock. McHenry would routinely call my father late at night to come down and take his inebriated father home.

Men.

ABL during happier days.

One of the many men's groups of which ABL was a part.

ABL with more crime-fighting men.

**ABL's second wedding.
His second wife Della is immediately to his left and his son
and my father on the far left of the image.**

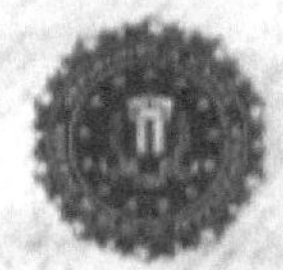

Federal Bureau of Investigation
United States Department of Justice
Washington, D. C.

May 26, 1955

Mr. A. B. Leckie
3410 Wilshire Boulevard
Los Angeles 36, California

Dear Mr. Leckie:

Thank you for your note of May 24.

I recall very well indeed the waitress
at the Ambassador Hotel Coffee Shop whom you
mentioned. It is always a pleasure for me
to see her when I am in Los Angeles and I
was glad to know that you had met and talked
with her.

Sincerely,

J. Edgar Hoover

**Letter to ABL from Hoover 16 years after his firing oozing
with possible double entendre.**

'The' mystery postcard addressed to ABL at the Tail o' the Cock and signed, "Love and kisses, Johnny".

But who was Johnny?

ABL and the mystery man resembling a young Jack Kerouac on the beach at Venice, California.

Chapter 9

(Not) Like Father, (Not) Like Son

During his Tail o' the Cock years, ABL's only child, my father, married his college sweetheart, my mother, Maryanne Hammatt. In a letter by ABL to his mother on December 30, 1959, he wrote, "Dear Mama, This little guy has had a December that he will not soon forget. No. 1 Bunny had his birthday on December 10. He heard that he had passed the California State Bar examination on December 14, and he was married Monday evening, December 21. My business has been extremely heavy, aside from all of these things, but with some help from outsiders, I have been able to hold my head up and carry along. I was with Bernie on each of these occasions. After all, he is all I've got, and being me, I did not spare the horses. I gave him and Maryanne their sterling silver set of eight place settings of six pieces each of the Royal Danish pattern and the chest. I know that they sincerely appreciated this gift. I had planned it with them some time ahead so that no one else would give them this particular gift ..."

He hilariously wrote, "When Bernie started to pull the veil up to kiss her at the altar, he certainly fumbled the ball. He was trying to get to Maryanne so fast, he almost wrecked her." He continued, "Bernie, with the wonderful speaking voice he has, could be heard in every corner of the church, and he spoke the marriage vows beautifully, as did Maryanne ... The reception was held at the Disneyland Hotel, which is a new addition to Disneyland ..." In the same letter, my grandfather touchingly wrote, "As a matter of fact, it was probably the happiest evening of my life."

In February 1939, a story in *The Philadelphia Inquirer* featured a small picture of my father as a six-year-old patting a dog. It appeared alongside a larger photo of his crime-fighting father with the funny headline "Son of Top Philadelphia G-Man Wants None of Dad's Work: Says, 'No, Thanks' to Edgar Hoover's Office. He Won't Follow in Father's Footsteps." The lives of a dad and a son.

My dad became a successful lawyer with renowned clients, but he never walked the hallways of the FBI. He did, on occasion, engage very intimately with certain elements of the National Security State, the details of which I will keep quiet for the moment, but all in all, watching my father morph increasingly into a stronger and stronger humanitarian person always heartened me. It was beautiful to behold his personal evolution into a truly caring man who valued Chileans, Pakistanis, or Nigerians as he did Americans. His selflessness just increased with each passing year. His generosity and kindness just grew. He was a sensitive and jolly man, and I miss him horribly.

My dad would chuckle whenever the 1938 article by Allen Will Harris came up in conversation. It highlighted not only ABL's prominence but also underscored the peak of ABL's presence in the FBI at that time. This 1938 article read, "America's youngsters won't believe it, but there's a Philadelphia six-year-old who scorned J. Edgar Hoover's invitation to be a G-Man. Of course, it was all in fun, but even at that cue would have expected 'Bunny' Leckie to have jumped at even the chance. As it was, he merely shuffled his feet nervously, said a falsetto, 'No, thanks,' and held his father's hand a bit more tightly. Naturally, there is a fact that explains Bunny's steadfast anti-G-Man policy. Father Leckie, better known as A. Bernard Leckie, is a special agent in charge of the Philadelphia bureau of the FBI, a rank which makes him one of the nation's leading crime investigation officials. And even at the moderately tender age of six, you can't blame a guy for knowing that his dad is in a mighty dangerous business. Tall, heavy-set, with a soft accent that can be traced to an Alabama boyhood, the local G-Man head always laughs when he tells of Bunny's answer to Hoover's job proposal. 'Give him time,' he says. 'I'm not sure, but I think he'll learn to love the work as much as I do. After all, FBI-ing calls for a grand combination of brain and brawn. Anyone who likes adventure likes the business.' When one mentions the fourteen G-Men who have died battling gangsters, Leckie is silent but not worried. After a thought, he replies that the spirit of the 607 agents is so good that none of them ever think about the possibility of death. 'Each day is a success if we come closer to solving the problem at hand,' he says. 'We haven't time to be frightened!' One reason why the death rate for federal agents has been relatively low is that each man must be an expert with a gas gun, pump shotgun, .351 rifle, 30-06 rifle, automatic, Thompson machine gun, and several other weapons. Under all sorts of weather conditions, the men go out into the fields once a month to practice shooting for their accuracy tests. Leckie credits part of the success of the Hoover clan to its freedom from political interference and part of the sound educational background each recruit must have. 'These G-Men are trained to use their heads for more than hatracks,' he says. 'Why, several years back, one of 'em went into the Tennessee mountains to get a hillbilly bank robber. He made friends with the village folk and played the violin so well at a barn dance that the fugitive's papa showed him the family hiding place.' That's the sort of 'fast track' Leckie would like Bunny to do someday. 'It's a good sign, this caution of his,' he argues proudly. 'The lad's learning, like any good G-Man, to size up a situation himself. Just wait til he gets started. I pity the gangsters.' But, of course, it doesn't take a Federal Bureau of Investigation official to recognize that as an everyday parental brag!"

Chapter IO

Della

In his final decade, ABL's work as an LA private eye flourished from his office at 5525 Wilshire Blvd. Though he would have competed with the likes of famed private investigator Fred Otash, clearly, he was one of the go-to snoops for Hollywood's finest. In contrast, his personal life painfully turned. He divorced his first wife, my nana, in March 1958. Later that year, in October, he rather suddenly married again in San Diego to none other than Della Sayre, one of Hoover's previous private secretaries. These rather central facts were kept from me for a long while, and I never knew any of this while growing up. For a time, their marriage seemed happy. Della sent three postcards to Mary Scott and John in October 1958. One is from the Cocoanut Grove Los Angeles Ambassador. On it, Della wrote, "I'm happy to be a Leckie. Our wedding was perfect. I wish you could have been here. Our love, Della & Bernard." Another card is from the Hotel Mark Hopkins in San Francisco, on which Della wrote, "This place is fabulous—and AB is wonderful. Love, Della." Another card came from Yosemite Valley.

Needless to say, Della's brief eight-month stint with ABL quickly turned sour and seemed to be fraught far more with misery than joy, as evidenced by a sad and highly revealing letter dated June 11, 1959, where Della expressed her boundless dissatisfaction with being married to a man more devoted to the bottle than to his new wife.

"Dear AB, I was very upset again last evening after talking to you. The mental, physical, and emotional turmoil of recent months has taken such a toll on me. I can't recuperate. It seems I'm exhausted, being upset so much about so many things. It seems to me for the last eight months, all I've done is share living quarters with you—not your life! You live to suit yourself—work when and where you please—frequent your favorite haunts—fraternize with your cronies—and when anything interferes with what you want to do and when you want to do it—that is shoved aside without any consideration by you! Whether it happens to be me—a job—or what have you? You are determined to suit yourself at any cost. And when you drink so much —so often—that you can't remember what you have said, and so at such times—it would seem to me for your own sake, if not for any other reason, it is time for you to pause and reflect—to take inventory, so to speak. You made many promises before we were married—most of which you quickly broke—without regard for anyone but yourself. Liquor seems the most important thing to you—I told you before we were married I would not try to compete with a strong drink! Liquor seems to befog you—your sense of values—your judgment. It certainly affects your memory. It's up to you as to whether or not you want me to share your present and your future. Let me know! Della." Whoa.

Another letter from Della to ABL six weeks later, on July 23, 1959, reveals she was seething even higher. She wrote, "I am not supposed to resent all the money you squander on your own appetites and the money you lavish entertaining others, in addition to the huge tips you give to inflate your ego ... besides your GIFTS. It is all I am entitled to—I suppose—the privilege of CRUMBS FROM YOUR TABLE, so to speak—if I happen to be at your table ..."

In a deposition of ABL carried out in connection with their divorce held on December 6, 1961, in LA, the well-known LA law firm Meserve, Mumper & Hughes represented ABL, the firm where my father later joined in his storied legal career, where his client roster ranged from stars on the LA Rams and New Orleans Saints NFL teams, to OJ Simpson, and even to the first well-known male porn star, John "The Wadd" Holmes. Among other things, ABL noted in the deposition that, "I have had a lot of bad health in the last two years, and my work has been farmed out to other investigators, a great deal of it ... As a matter of fact, in recent months, practically all of it has gone out because I have been in the Good Samaritan Hospital for eight days not long ago, and I have been sick with this cold for six weeks, plus rheumatism in my hands and wrists, and the doctors tell me I may not be able to drive very much longer. I have whiplash in my neck, and I have sclerosis and diabetes." He hurt in one way; she in another. It proved to be a horrible match.

A month later, in a deposition of Della Sayre Leckie held on January 9, 1962, she interestingly indicated that she left the FBI in 1946, seven years after ABL. Referencing his painful departure from the land of Hoover, Della noted that, "I left under much more favorable circumstances than Mr. Leckie." In response to a question as to whether she ever stayed in the same apartment as ABL in 1959, she replied, "I was refused admittance to that apartment. My husband had a man, and heaven knows who else moved into that apartment with him." What was she alluding to?

In another deposition involving her contestation of ABL's will, four years later, on January 14, 1966, she noted that there was a reconciliation of sorts in 1962 wherein she and ABL "had sexual intercourse more than just one time." The January 9 deposition featured many heated exchanges and was rather unruly. After informing the lawyers that she had been bedridden for six months due to a heart attack, she claimed to have worked for ABL during their marriage without being paid, noting, "My husband took in thirty-six thousand dollars [almost four hundred thousand today] during the year 1959 when I worked as his secretary without pay."

When asked about ABL's daily activities, one lawyer queried Della, "Do you know where your husband was on that day?"

She replied, "No, I do not. If he was in Los Angeles, it was probably at the Tail o' the Cock." She then retorted to the opposing lawyer, "Thank God I am not married to you. It was bad enough to be married to Mr. Leckie." She was not happy. She told them all about his problems with alcohol, noting, "I wonder if he would be interested in how much my husband spent on liquor. I wonder if he wants to read my husband's love letters and see I had no knowledge of where my husband was.

"My husband never seemed to be prepared about anything.

"My husband usually was drunk, so what he said half the time was not complimentary.

"I lived with him until September 1959 when he insisted I go to San Diego, after which he abandoned me ... He was so deceitful about everything else ... He was at home, drunk most of the time."

Della wrote the following in a note to ABL on May 9, 1962, just three months before his death: "Dear AB, Your treatment of me was shocking and disappointing. You apparently condoned and agreed with your attorney's actions and he with yours. I was shocked and surprised to learn of the irregularities. I feel I am entitled to compensation for my wedding gifts, my personal effects, and other articles that you retained and refused to return. I shall expect to hear from you by return mail so that an appropriate settlement can be accomplished in your best interests, Della."

In yet another letter from Della dated August 18, 1962, to the Pierce Brothers Mortuary following ABL's death, she noted, "My stepson's wife [my mother] advised an autopsy had been performed, but it would take six months to ascertain the cause of death." Despite their divorce finalization long before ABL's death, she signed the letter, "Very truly yours, Della S. Leckie, Mrs. A.B. Leckie, 1918 Sunset Boulevard, San Diego 3, California," clearly attempting to give the impression she was still owed something.

Their marriage only lasted a few short months. Again, it makes me wonder if it was true love or just another fake marriage to deceive the public and hide the true sexuality of a male partner. Such couples often had children to add to the deception, and examples from recent history abound. As a straight man with immense love for my countless gay friends of all genders all over the world, I would have loved it if ABL were gay and able to be open about it. I ask these questions not to undermine his reputation or posthumously "out" him in any way. I mention it now only to disclose how, if it is true, it may have contributed to or even have been the primary reason behind his heavy drinking. Perhaps he sought to escape an immutable truth in an alcohol-induced haze, unable to live the life he was meant to live.

It has always moved me when men and women who were so obviously part of the LGBTQIA+ community felt so compelled by the cruelty of society to actively try to hide it, living through deception and denial in ways that must have devastated them every single day. I have witnessed this numerous times. Rock Hudson, the famous actor and sex symbol extraordinaire, suffered this fate and lived most, if not all, of his life with this open secret having never been shared with the public. Hudson had season tickets to USC football games at the LA Coliseum in the 1960s and 1970s in the row right in front of my family's season tickets. He would sit inches away from me every time the Trojans had a home game. I couldn't believe my luck. A star right in front of me! Even though I didn't understand the whole idea of being gay at such a young age, as I began to understand it, Hudson's noticeably cautious behavior with his fellow fans started to make sense. I still vividly remember him reaching out to a man on either his left or right, just about to hug him after a big play, only to quickly pull back. It dawned on him that in 1960s and 70s LA, such an act was still dangerous and could threaten his career.

A letter from ABL's brother Dulin to my father from March 1963 noted that their sister, Mary Scott, "told me about this woman filing a claim. Bernard [ABL] never promised her any such thing; when he was here in May 1962, he told me he was so happy that he was rid of her and that she had signed and accepted a full settlement sometime in February 1962. He also said he had the best time at home in May 1962 that he had had in a very long time since he had no worries and that you had told him just before leaving there that he would be a grandfather. I have never seen him in such good spirits. So, I know he felt sure he had gotten rid of her finally and for all time."

After ABL died, Della made claims for a large portion of his estate, filing for fifty thousand dollars [five hundred thousand today], arguing that he had promised it to her. A 1966 deposition asked, point blank, "He wanted to resume your marriage?"

Her answer, "Yes, he did. He had cried, and I knew that he was not a man who ever wept. When I saw that he was so distressed, I felt he was really sincere, and I agreed that we would reconcile ... I told you that we reconciled, we lived together as man and wife, and we both agreed that we were husband and wife." As a result of these highly dubious claims, which have become family lore, my honest, law-abiding, non-religious dad started praying, losing weight, and suffering anguish. The absurd legal battle, which he eventually and inevitably won, wore on year after year due to seven years of pestering by Sayre's lawyers and others. Though she lost the case and never got her hands on the fifty thousand dollars she was seeking, Della lived a good, long life, passing away only in January 2008 at the age of ninety-six.

Though he was not rich and did not own a home at the time of his death, ABL's wealth primarily consisted of a few stocks and bonds, and he lived in a middle-class apartment in West LA. Nevertheless, his career remained as active and high-level as ever in the early 1960s.

According to the report of inheritance tax appraiser, ABL's net worth at the time of his death was $67,856.97. After deductions for funeral costs and outstanding debts of $9,319.83, his estate totaled precisely $58,537.14. By the time the estate had been settled in 1967, following the prolonged lawsuit filed by Della, the value of the stock holdings had increased to almost $110,000 [around one million dollars today]. In the end, after years of challenging the will and seeking a huge portion of ABL's estate, the court declared that Della had no interest in the estate by judicial order on January 3, 1967, by the Superior Court of the State of California for the County of Los Angeles.

As we will shortly see, ABL's death, occurring just three years after divorcing Della, raised numerous suspicions. His death was reported as having several causes and given what he was up to at the time, suspicion seems a sensible response to his unexpected death. When considering the very real possibility that he may have been murdered, we must first consider motive. Who could have wanted him killed and why? Who stood to benefit and how? What did he know or do that would have made someone, or people, or even an institution, so afraid that they would risk getting caught by killing a former FBI agent known as a shrewd little sleuth? Perhaps, too, we need to consider others besides the obvious suspects who might have felt so aggrieved, so betrayed, so hurt that they might have risked all, not only for the money that would presumably be acquired but also simply to act out a premeditated crime of passion not involving outright physical violence but using poison or other tools to bring about ABL's premature demise. We may never know.

Chapter II

Marilyn

It is not surprising that ABL received a call in July 1962 to investigate the life of the world's most famous woman after playing central roles in the FBI, Pearl Harbor, the UN's founding, the McCarthy trials, finding Howard Hughes' hiding places *twice*, marrying Hoover's personal secretary, and acting as a private detective for countless Hollywood bigwigs—including Marlon Brando and many other well-known stars—and befriending many of Hollywood's finest, including actor Jack Webb who made the famous crime-fighting US TV show *Dragnet* later in his career. Strangely, for a known right-winger like ABL, he associated with numerous progressive clients. Marilyn had strong feelings "about civil rights, for black equality, as well as her admiration for what was being done in China, her anger at redbaiting and McCarthyism, and her hatred of J. Edgar Hoover."[33] It wasn't shared political views, clearly, that led her to contact this well-known super sleuth.

Though closer in time than the earlier parts of his life, the final

---

[33]Anthony Summers, Goddess: The Secret Lives of Marilyn Monroe (Updated Edition), Weidenfeld & Nicolson, 2022, p. 373.

portion of his days are blurrier but even more compelling than anything that preceded it. Some things are clear and certain, especially the big-picture themes, but some of the more tangential elements are less so. We know for sure, for instance, that throughout at least the month of July 1962, and perhaps earlier, ABL had a significant involvement in Marilyn Monroe's life. According to my father, Marilyn hired ABL to find out "who it was or what it was that is terrorizing me." ABL's brother, Earl Leckie, also told his son, Chuck, the same thing—Marilyn hired him to figure out who was watching her.

My mother recalls it differently, and though she confirms ABL's involvement in the intricate details of Marilyn's life, she remembered that he was hired not by Marilyn but by the father of actress Terry Moore—who was allegedly having an affair with Robert F. Kennedy (RFK), the attorney general and brother of President John F. Kennedy (JFK). If this is true, ostensibly, Moore's father probably wanted to know if RFK was also seeing Marilyn at the same time, in effect two-timing her, his wife, and who knows how many others. Moore was married five times and claimed to have also been Howard Hughes' partner during the 1950s and 1960s, so the connection to ABL could have also been due to his links with Hughes. Terry Moore is still alive, 96 years young. I tried contacting her through her website to see if she had any information to share, but alas, I received no reply.

I believe my mother's recollection of ABL's involvement with Terry Moore is correct but not related to Marilyn; rather, it was connected to ABL's engagements with Howard Hughes. It is far more likely that Moore's father hired ABL to seek out Hughes again, bearing in mind that Moore was, indeed, allegedly married to the world's richest man.

The pathways leading to Marilyn's life and her home located at 12305 Fifth Helena Avenue in Brentwood may be open to dispute. However, everyone is in consensus about the destination and what ABL must have uncovered.

The early 1960s were an extraordinary time in countless ways in the US, not the least of which involved the hope and intrigue surrounding the Kennedy Administration. The alleged dalliances by

JFK and his attorney general and brother, RFK, both of whom were widely known to have been sexually involved with a range of high-profile women, would have been well known in certain circles. As Anthony Summers and others have meticulously documented, Marilyn Monroe had affairs with both President Kennedy and Robert. JFK's reputation with women was so widely known that his close friends referred, rather distastefully, to him as Shafty.[34]

For decades following her death until the present day, the lives of these three would be forever linked. Precisely how ABL's life fits in remains incredibly mysterious. If he worked for Marilyn at the time of both his and her death, just a day and a half apart, what precisely was he doing? Was he spying on Marilyn's spies or trying to find dirt that could hurt her? What could the role have been of that other famous LA private eye, Fred Otash? ABL must have known him and perhaps felt professionally jealous of a man of similar stature who received a lot more attention. Among other things, Teamsters leader Jimmy Hoffa hired Otash to work with surveillance expert Bernard Spindel, spying on Marilyn to entrap their real enemies, the Kennedys. Ultimately, they placed recording devices at Peter Lawford's house, which allegedly recorded JFK and Marilyn having sex.

"In the hands of Spindel, with his connections to the Mob and Mob associates—to Hoffa and on occasion Giancana—the recordings posed a tangible threat to the President. Kennedy's involvement with Marilyn, which had always been folly, became more so as the months passed, for she was disintegrating emotionally."[35]

Add to this the well-known Mafia figures Sam Giancana and Johnny Roselli, who were also watching the Kennedys and thus Marilyn. Giancana was perhaps most famous for his outburst during an arrest by the FBI that, "I know all about the Kennedys, and Phyllis (his girlfriend at the time) knows a lot more about the Kennedys and one of these days we are going to tell all … You lit a fire tonight that will never go out. You'll rue the day."[36]

---

[34]Id, p. 307.

[35]Id, p. 349.

[36]Id, p. 343.

Finding yet another possible link to ABL, Summers discovered that, "Roselli had been recruited by the CIA for the infamous series of plots to assassinate Fidel Castro. The agency would not break off contact with the Mafia, and with Roselli and Giancana in particular, until 1963."[37]

When people asked if he believed in the rumors of Marilyn and the Kennedys, Chuck Leckie told me he asked ABL's son, my father, what he thought, to which my dad famously replied, "If a man's ass is seen going over the fence, you can assume he was messing around."

Not only did JFK know Marilyn Monroe since 1951[38], but he was also involved with Judith Campbell Exner[39], the first woman to publicly admit to an affair with the president and also engaged with Mafia head, Giancana. This exposed the leader of the free world to the serious threat of blackmail.

Addressing Exner's role in the broader controversies surrounding the Kennedy and Monroe saga, investigative reporter extraordinaire Seymour Hersh, in his widely heralded book *The Dark Side of Camelot*, noted that, "In August 1962, with the FBI watching, Judith Campbell Exner's apartment in Los Angeles was broken into by two brothers whose get-away car was rented by their father—the chief of security of the General Dynamics Corporation, one of America's largest defense contractors. Three months later, General Dynamics—everyone's second choice—was awarded a $6.5 billion contract for the experimental TFX jet fighter."[40] Well, that's intriguing.

ABL left the FBI in 1939 but remained in regular contact with Hoover, who still headed the agency into the 1970s. Hoover publicly hated Kennedy, as did Hoffa and Giancana. People linked to the FBI and the Mob, therefore, all watched how Marilyn lived her life—and with whom. The Kennedys were terrified that Marilyn might speak out as she began to accept that her days with the Kennedy brothers were over, and they likely watched her too. In a way, it doesn't matter *who*

---

[37]Id, p. 342.

[38]Id, p. 311.

[39]For a good overview, see Liz Smith, "The Exner Files," *Vanity Fair*, January 1997.

[40]Seymour M. Hersh, *The Dark Side of Camelot*, Little, Brown and Co, 1997, p. 295.

hired ABL to play the sleuth because no matter who it was and what its objectives were, my grandfather would have witnessed and known all of this first-hand. He knew who was watching Marilyn and more than a few intimate details of her life.

There are so many twists and turns to this story that recounting it all here would be impossible, but suffice it to say that Seymour Hersh had it right when he wrote, "Yet, when Marilyn Monroe died, both [Kennedy] brothers were forced to use the FBI to cover up their affairs with the actress."[41] Hersh confirmed the mass surveillance carried out at Marilyn's house: "It has been clear for some time now that Monroe came under electronic surveillance during the Kennedy presidency. Interviews with private detectives and technicians leave no doubt of it. Confusion remains, however, as to who commissioned the bugging and who received the 'take.' Teamsters' leader Hoffa, a prime target of the Kennedy Justice Department, almost certainly received some compromising material. He said as much to fellow prisoners when he later went to jail, and his attorney, William Buffalino, confirmed it in a 1990 interview. Some bugging, meanwhile, may have been commissioned by the mobster Giancana."[42] Some might have been done by none other than master spy ABL, using all the tricks of the trade he'd learned during the McCarthy years and beyond. Another in-depth book about Monroe's death confirms different perspectives.

"Marilyn's house had been well and truly bugged ... Wiretapper Bernard Spindel was commissioned to record Robert Kennedy in both the Lawford beach house [in reference to actor and Kennedy clan family member through marriage, Peter Lawford] and Marilyn's house on Fifth Helena Drive. Bernard Spindel, however, was not the only one listening in on what was happening at the Lawford and Monroe houses. On the grounds that Robert Kennedy was considered a security risk for conducting an affair with Marilyn, the FBI kept the couple under surveillance. In fact, she qualified for surveillance on her own, as the FBI had raised a 105 file on her regarding 'foreign counter-intelligence matters.' Marilyn had obtained a reputation for talking to

---

[41]Id, photo captions mid-book, 31, 32.
[42]Id, p. 343.

all the wrong people, and the concept of the attorney general talking to Marilyn was dynamite to the FBI. They had their bugs and taps in place and listened avidly. There is little doubt that Hoover gave all of the material collected from the Marilyn and Kennedy affair personal attention, and much of it finished up in his notorious files. And even this was not all. The CIA, for much the same reason as the FBI, had placed a wire. Agency members were sworn enemies of both John and Robert Kennedy, and it is disturbing that even if the agents on the ground were not personally involved in the hatred campaign, the tapes' content was transmitted upward, increasing the risk of them falling into vindictive hands. The CIA at this time was a rogue elephant, controlled by no higher authority, and it was quite on the cards that personnel would quickly make the tape product available to the Kennedy clan's bitterest enemies."[43]

As we remember Marilyn Monroe over sixty years after her death, the stories that swirl about her final days remain captivating and, in many ways, hair-raising, even without my grandfather's involvement. That such a young and beautiful woman would die allegedly by her own hand at such an early age under such mysterious circumstances makes the story compelling. Increasing speculation that she was murdered raises the stakes yet further. She was romantically involved with both Kennedys and a Mob boss, and she was married, for a third time, to celebrated playwright Arthur Miller, the creator of masterpieces like *Death of a Salesman* and *The Crucible*. Miller had been investigated during the Hollywood McCarthy purges, in which ABL played a central role, further complicating matters. Her doctor, Hyman Engelberg, was also investigated during the McCarthy hearings. Additionally, ABL working at Lockheed in the 1940s at the same time as both Robert Mitchum and Marilyn Monroe only pushes the intrigue meter higher.[44]

The involvement of the FBI and Hoover in the case again must make one wonder. One author specifically noted that, "At this perilous time in history, J. Edgar Hoover received another confidential

---

[43]Matthew Smith, *The Men Who Murdered Marilyn*, Bloomsbury, 1996, p. 107 and 116.

memorandum from the FBI office in Mexico City headed 'MARILYN MONROE—SECURITY MATTER—C [communist].' Dated July 13, 1962—just three weeks prior to Marilyn's death—the document, withheld from the FBI's Monroe file, survived in highly censored form in the FBI files of both Peter Lawford and Frederick Vanderbilt Field. Under the Freedom of Information appeals process, the FBI told attorney James Lesar that the source of the censored information in the Monroe memorandum was an informant. The CIA had requested that the FBI not reveal the informant's name. However, the FBI disclosed to Lesar that the source was someone who knew both Field and Monroe and had recently been in private conversation with both of them."[45]

According to Summers, perhaps the premier expert on the life of Marilyn Monroe, she allegedly went to Mexico for an abortion after becoming pregnant—rumor has it—from either JFK or his brother.[46] For a long period of time during their affair, Marilyn thought she would marry Robert Kennedy and become a formal part of Camelot. Summers noted that, "At the time of Marilyn's visit to Mexico City, FBI agents there were paying constant attention to a group of some several dozen expatriate Americans. They watched especially members of the Hollywood Ten, filmmakers whose careers had been destroyed during the McCarthy communist-hunting era of the 1950s, and other leftists. When Marilyn had been befriended during her stay by 'silver spoon communist' Fred Vanderbilt Field, that had attracted intense FBI interest."[47]

The same FBI report from July 13, 1962, noted that, "something

---

[44]"Marilyn's physician, Hyman Engelberg, had well-documented communist connections. His name appeared on the register of the Communist People's Educational Centre, where he taught late in 1937. As a speaker or supporter, Engelberg has political sympathies, which were easily identified. At the US House Committee on Un-American Activities hearings in 1954, he was identified as a member of the Communist Party." Source: Id, p. 124.

[45]Donald H. Wolfe, *The Assassination of Marilyn Monroe*, Little, Brown and Company, 1998, p. 434.

[46]Supra, Summers, p. 417.

[47]Id, p. 454.

the unnamed source had heard direct from Marilyn herself. She was quoted as saying she had 'lunched at the Peter Lawford's with President Kennedy' just a few days previously. She was very pleased, as she had asked the president a lot of socially significant questions concerning the morality of atomic testing ... Subject's views are very positively and concisely leftist; however, if she is being actively used by the Communist Party, it is not general knowledge among those working with the movement in Los Angeles.'"[48]

Hundreds of books have been written in the past six decades about the life and times of Marilyn Monroe—tens of thousands of pages of often real and difficult-to-understand facts also often infused with degrees of conspiracy, paranoia, and even a bit of incredulousness that such things were ever published at all. Not having any particular interest in Ms. Monroe, I only began reading more than twenty credible accounts of her life due to her connection to ABL. I focused especially on the analyses of her death to see if there was any link between the two mysterious deaths. Given the vast amount of material available, a very lengthy book dedicated to just the three-day period immediately prior to and following both of their deaths would be a very real possibility.

But since that is outside my range, if we distil that week into a few paragraphs based on the most serious research since then, the story has enough verifiable facts to conclude that the first week of August 1962 was a time of extraordinary events. ABL snooped around her house, carrying out her remit to him to find out "who it was or what it was that was terrifying me." My father repeatedly recounted it to me, and my mother and my father's cousin Chuck verified it. We know for certain he worked for her in the months leading up to their deaths. The real questions thus become: What did he uncover? What did he find out? Who was it?

From the findings of Summers, Hersh, Smith, Wolfe, and many others, as well as from countless official documents, we know that Marilyn and the Kennedys were very close. In her mind, she believed that she would one day soon become the new Mrs. Robert F. Kennedy.

---

[48]Id, p. 457.

RFK visited Marilyn in her home in the days leading up to her death, conversing with her to the effect that marriage was not in the cards, the relationships between RFK and JFK were finished, and that she should tell no one that anything had happened—even though many friends and journalists knew that a lot had happened.

As Anthony Summers recounted, "Some hinted darkly that Marilyn knew too much, that she and her diary had become too explosive, that the Kennedys—or some shadowy agency on their behalf—did away with her. Others speculated that Marilyn, already linked to the Kennedys by gossip, was killed by the brothers' enemies to ensure an explosion of scandal that would destroy the presidency. Which enemies?"[49]

Others thought it was the Mafia or the Cubans or perhaps even Hoover himself, who, by doing so, would have held the ultimate "dirt" perpetually over the heads of the family he hated so much, the Kennedys.

If we consider the possibility of murder in terms of motive, we now know the remarkable fact that Marilyn was secretly sleeping with both JFK and RFK. She clearly had the power or naïve misfortune to bring down the presidency. In political realms, it doesn't get more threatening than that. According to some sources, the night Marilyn died, Robert was in San Francisco, preparing to speak to the American Bar Association. He allegedly clandestinely flew to LA that night, assisted by his friend, actor Peter Lawford. Lawford allegedly told Marilyn that her affairs with the Kennedys were over and no more visits to the White House would be on the agenda.[50] Some now believe the suicide story was fabricated and that she was murdered in a rather ghoulish manner.[51]

Interestingly, the facts show that beyond any government agencies or others that may have been spying on Marilyn at the time of her death, private investigators and detectives were also involved. ABL must have fully known at a professional level these private eyes, including the famed Fred Otash and Bernard Spindel, among others. He surely saw them as competitors in the relatively small world of

---

[49]Id, p. 479.

private eyes in LA. According to Summers again, "Close associates of wiretapper Bernard Spindel, whom Teamsters' boss Hoffa reportedly hired to get information on Marilyn and the Kennedy brothers, offered a troubling account of Marilyn's final hours. According to Spindel's associate Paris Theodore, the wiretapper later played him some forty minutes of tape-recording covering activity at Marilyn's home on the day she died. The recording reflected two visits to Marilyn's house by Robert Kennedy … Marilyn was demanding an explanation as to why Kennedy was not going to marry her."[52] Historical records show that Otash was less involved prior to her death than afterward, "Otash, Wilson, and other associates were specialists for hire. There were only a handful of them in Los Angeles in 1962, and on this occasion—great historical irony—the new mission called for a cover-up *on behalf of the Kennedys*."[53]

I have no idea whether that is all true or not, but I know ABL

---

[50]*Supra*, Wolfe: "The attorney general was in California at the time, to address the American Bar Association and to take a vacation with the family. A mass of testimony, supported in the eighties by that of Peter Lawford, suggests Kennedy flew to Los Angeles on August 4 for a showdown with Monroe. According to Lawford, who admitted accompanying his brother-in-law to Monroe's house, there was an ugly quarrel. "Marilyn," he said, allowed how first thing Monday morning, she was going to call a press conference and tell the world about the treatment she had suffered at the hands of the Kennedy brothers. Bobby became livid. In no uncertain terms, he told her she was going to have to leave both Jack and himself alone—no more telephone calls, no letters, nothing."(p. 347) "According to Lawford, the row ended with hysteria from Monroe, a struggle in which she was subdued, then an urgent call for help to her psychiatrist, Dr. Ralph Greenson. Dr. Greenson did come over, believed he had calmed Monroe down, and went off to dinner. It was he, according to the official account, who would be summoned by the housekeeper of the files in the early hours of the following morning to find Monroe dead in bed. Yet, statements by police officers, ambulance men, the housekeeper of the files, doctors, and others suggest the following scenario: After desperate calls by Monroe to the Lawford beach house, Kennedy and his brother-in-law returned to her home. They found the actress either dead or dying and phoned for an ambulance. One or both of them may have joined the ambulance on a last-hope drive to a hospital—only to turn it around when it became clear Monroe was dead. The body was then replaced in the bed, and the president's brother left town rapidly the way he had arrived, by helicopter and aircraft. Dr. Greenson confirmed privately, years later, that Robert Kennedy was present that night and that an ambulance was called."(p. 347).

carried out his investigations for a few weeks. He must have discovered more than a few compromising things that could have put him in danger. According to a quote in Summer's book, when asked to tell what he knew about Marilyn's demise, her psychiatrist, Ralph Greenson, famously, simply said, "I can't tell the whole story ... Talk to Robert Kennedy."[54]

Marilyn famously once said, "I know a lot of secrets about what has gone on in Washington ... dangerous ones ... something shocking, something that will one day shock the whole world."[55]

It is widely known that Marilyn officially died as a result of "probable suicide," according to the autopsy and death certificate. In a manner very similar to how my father described the autopsy of his father by the same LA County Coroner's Office, Summers noted that, "There was a coroner's investigation, and it was flawed. There was a police investigation, and there was a cover-up."[56] Summers added, "The circumstances of Marilyn's death, which very much involved the Kennedys, were deliberately covered up."[57]

Much of the alleged cover-up is based on phone calls made to and

---

[51]Id., Wolfe makes the shocking allegation that: "The evidence points to premeditated homicide. In the presence of Bobby Kennedy, she was injected with enough barbiturate to kill fifteen people." (p. 463). While according to Matthew Smith in *The Men Who Murdered Marilyn*, Bloomsbury, 1996: John Miner told me that Ralph Greenson was deeply distressed by Marilyn's death and particularly by the idea that she had committed suicide. "I can tell you without doubt," said John Miner, "Greenson did not believe that. He did not believe she had committed suicide." (p. 103) "John Miner wants Marilyn's body to be exhumed for tests on the lining of the lower colon, or large intestine. This will please Dr. Noguchi, who will happily collaborate in any new investigation. Miner believes that because she is buried in a crypt, there will be sufficient tissue to show that the drugs were administered by way of enema."(p. 105). "... so it can be said with confidence that injection was not the means of death." (p. 100).

[52]Supra, Summers, p. 521.

[53]Id, p. 513.

[54]Id, p. iii.

[55]Id, p. 453.

[56]Id, p. 469.

[57]Id, p. 481.

from Marilyn's two phones. One of these phones was pink for normal calls, and then another white phone was reserved for what Summers refers to as "specially privileged." Summers noted that, "The police list of calls covering her last days, August 1 to 4, show only three calls. One on Friday was to Norman Rosten in New York, and the other two were to places in Los Angeles."[58]

Intriguingly, ABL could be one of those two calls. He worked for her and died with her private number—the white phone—in his back pocket. We know that, but what happened at the time was clearly designed to keep whomever she was speaking to a very secret matter indeed.

Summers explained, "A former FBI agent, James Doyle, revealed to me that the FBI has indeed intervened to ensure that the records of Marilyn's final phone calls remained beyond the reach of other investigators. His knowledge was first hand … His certainty that the orders came from Robert Kennedy or the president himself suggests that the brothers knew the incalculable damage they could suffer were the phone records made public. To contain the damage, they were forced to turn for help to FBI Director Hoover. The brothers would forever be indebted to him."[59]

Perhaps one or both of the missing calls were, indeed, made to Bobby Kennedy, as has been alleged. "On the morning of Marilyn's death, when the chief of detectives, Thad Brown, had been summoned to headquarters because of a 'problem,' he had been about to spend the day with the assistant chief of the regional Intelligence Division of the Treasury Department, Virgil Crabtree. The problem, Brown told Crabtree, was that a piece of crumpled paper had been found in Marilyn's bedclothes. It bore a telephone number at the White House."[60] Others recalled that, "Bobby Kennedy's telephone number was on the nightstand by her bed."[61]

We know for certain that ABL was spying on and for Marilyn and

---

[58]Id, p. 493.
[59]Id, pp. 494-495.
[60]Id, p. 496.
[61]Id, pp. 496-7.

those around her in the month prior to his death—and that her death took place within thirty-six hours of his in the same town in homes just a fifteen-minute drive apart. Both deaths were suspicious, and to me, this painful fact makes the sad ending to this family story even more shattering. Could the referred to secret FBI informant have been ABL? Did what he knew about what she knew get them both killed? Was he exposed to such a degree that someone, an agency, or an organization found it necessary to quiet an expendable ex-FBI agent forever?

Among others, the famous investigator and attorney John W. Miner, a former LA County deputy district attorney, believed that the official cause of death—listed on her death certificate as "probable suicide" due to acute barbiturate poisoning following an autopsy by LA Coroner Dr. Thomas Noguchi—was untenable and untrue. Miner asserted that Marilyn Monroe had also been murdered. In a February 25, 2011, *LA Times* article by Dennis McLellan, published at the time of Miner's death at the age of ninety-two, and reiterating Miner's conviction that Monroe had been murdered, noted that "the autopsy report said that 'the stomach is almost completely empty. No residue of the pills is noted.'" It also noted, "The toxic level was high; she would have had to take sixty to seventy pills." The case was so suspicious that Miner and others urged the authorities to exhume Marilyn's body to reinvestigate the cause of her death, but the cause of death officially remained probable suicide, and no one carried out a new autopsy.

In March 2007, just shy of forty-five years after Marilyn's death, a detailed three-page report became public for the first time, suggesting that RFK and Monroe were having an affair and that he was aware of and perhaps even involved in a plan to "induce suicide." The report noted that, "The allegations suggest that the thirty-six-year-old actress, who had a history of staging attention-seeking suicide attempts, was deliberately given the means to fake another suicide on August 4, 1962, but was allowed to die as she sought help." The document was forwarded to the FBI on October 19, 1964, by "an unnamed former special agent" working for then democrat governor of California, Pat

Brown.[62] It noted the FBI's surveillance for years, creating a file over fourteen hundred pages long, including a four-page redacted memo (with the exception of her name).[63]

In reference to the 1982 decision by the Los Angeles district attorney to reopen inquiries into a case that had never ceased to be the subject of rumor and controversy, his brief was limited. Was there sufficient evidence to open a criminal investigation? Could Monroe have been murdered? After four months, the DA was advised that the evidence failed "to support any theory of criminal conduct." The case was not re-opened.

So, if she was murdered, as many believe, or even induced to commit suicide, who was responsible? No one has ever been charged or convicted, and the case officially remains a suicide, but several names have been suggested as possible culprits behind different causes of death. Some might say that it's the Kennedys, of course, trying desperately to protect the presidency and family dynasty. Others may believe that it was Hoover and the FBI trying to get dirt on the Kennedys by killing her and blaming it on them. Additional suspects include opposing elements within the US government who wanted to beat Hoover to the news. Perhaps it was the Cuban exiles from the failed Bay of Pigs illegal US invasion of Cuba. Maybe it's the Mob. And then again, it could be no one; Marilyn really did simply commit suicide. Who knows?

Let's assume for a moment that ABL dialed that private number of hers on the night of August 2, 1962. The phone rang three times, then Marilyn answered. The conversation could have gone something like this:

"Hello?"

"Marilyn, it's Bunny. How are you?"

"Why, hello, Bunny. It's nice to hear a friendly voice on the phone for once. I have had so many painful calls in recent days; it's such a relief to hear your voice. You still have a slight Southern accent, as I'm sure you know, and it really is soothing."

---

[62]www.theage.com.au/news/world/kennedy-lonk-to-monroes-death, March 17, 2007.
[63]*Sydney Morning Herald*, 17 March, 2007.

"Well, that sure is sweet of you to say, Marilyn. I miss the South sometimes, but as we both know, LA has its charms. Less charming, however, and certainly less soothing is what I have to tell you tonight."

Immediately her chest tightened, and she quickly looked over at her dressing table for her "relaxing pills" as she called them. She couldn't immediately spot any, so she took a deep breath, tugged on her hair with one hand, and began digging the fingers of her other hand (with which she was holding the phone) into her palm as much as she could. Then she asked, "OK, Bunny. Tell me. What is it?"

"Marilyn, remember that you asked me to find out who it was or what it was that was terrorizing you?"

"Mmmhhhmmm."

"Well, I always had my suspicions, but now I know for sure. Shall we meet so I can give you my full report? It makes for rather stunning reading, so the sooner you are fully informed, the better, I think, in my professional opinion."

"Oh, Bunny, I'd love to meet, but I really can't just now, but I'm dying to know what you found out because I just can't stand it anymore. I feel like I'm going crazy. Can you please just tell me now?"

ABL thought about it and concluded that whatever he might say was already known to the more dangerous elements involved. If they had wanted to do anything nefarious to either him or Marilyn, they would have done so already. Perhaps it was a bit risky and even more reckless, but as time was of the essence, he concurred. And what he told her shocked her to her very core.

We may never know if Marilyn simply committed suicide on her own simply because she couldn't handle the pressures of being who she was. She wouldn't be the first to die in this manner. But let's permit her friend Robert Mitchum, who knew her for decades and who also knew ABL, have the final word: "I find it difficult to accept the suicide ruling on Marilyn's death. She was a confused, troubled lady who, confronted with living the life of an artificial stranger, felt inadequate to the demands of deportment expected of her but was never morose or despondent. I never saw her take a drink and know nothing of any association with pills."[64]

Despite all the evidence, we may never know if Marilyn was murdered or not, though a growing number of voices believe that to be far more likely than the authorities' suicide conclusion. If she was murdered, we can be pretty sure that whoever killed the world's most beautiful woman to silence her may have also killed a real-life Forrest Gump just a day before, a man who knew the very same secrets—and probably many more—and who may have shared these with her, my granddad: Arthur Bernard Leckie.

---

[64]Supra, Smith, p. 2.

Chapter 12

So Many Ways to Die

ABL spent the evening with my parents on August 1, 1962, where at one point, according to my mother, he danced around the room celebrating with immense joy that he was about to become a grandfather for the first time, in moving reference to my pending birth three months later, dancing around the living room singing, "I'm going to be a grandpa. Yippee!" He was happy, dancing, and singing, and seemingly, just as Marilyn, had everything to live for, as I, a six-month-old fetus, bobbed around in my mother's amniotic fluid, suspended in a state of semi-consciousness, taking in the vocal sounds of ABL, unknowingly feeling his essence, soaking up the spirit of this man just inches away—the first and last time I was close to him.

Less than two days later, ABL was found dead in his Beverly Grove apartment at 8561 Colgate Avenue on August 3, 1962, the front door agape, his death totally unexpected—and unsatisfactorily explained.

A lot of suspicion surrounded his untimely demise at the age of fifty-seven, and in various documents—his death certificate, newspaper accounts, obituaries, and others—surrounding his death, it was attributed to a range of different causes, including (1) diabetes mellitus, (2) a short illness, (3) a collapse, and (4) alcoholism. I'm thinking about a fifth and perhaps more likely explanation: murder. One of the many newspaper articles announcing his death quite specifically asserted that, "He collapsed as he rose from bed to answer the telephone" but did not indicate where this information came from. We know that a mystery man named Carlos with whom he was living would be the first to ask—if we only knew who he was. This could be true, just the sad end to an eventful life.

My generally very trusting lawyerly dad, who had seen everything LA had to offer, both good and especially bad, and who was anything but a believer in conspiracy theories, told me more than once that he believed that his father was, indeed, murdered. He told me over and over again that the investigation into his father's death was incomplete, botched, sloppy, error-ridden, and unprofessionally done. I attempted to access the autopsy report from the LA County Coroner's office to have a look for myself, but they failed to reply to my request.

If, as is alleged by some, Marilyn died on August 4, 1962 from an accidental overdose, an induced overdose, an involuntary enema filled with barbiturates, or even at the hands of another human being, then it is certainly within the realms of possibility that a man known to have diabetes could have been forcibly injected with overdose levels of insulin, say underneath his fingernails, and no one would have ever noticed. He could have been suffocated by a pillow, and no one would have known the difference. Some form of non-traceable poison could have been put into what was to become his final bottle of Early Times. The possibilities abound.

ABL was known around town, most certainly so in police, intelligence, and surveillance circles. His loose lips at the Tail o' the Cock after a bottle of whisky surely must have caused a few ripples of concern in this secretive milieu. If so many people and institutions spied on Marilyn at the same time, as is certainly the case, then each of them would have not only known what was going on in her life—but also who else was secretly peeking into it. After all of his experience in the FBI, his edgy and ongoing relationship with Hoover, his involvement with the McCarthy trials, and his right-wing leanings, ABL surely could have made enough enemies throughout his career. If he knew everything and others with the power and intent to kill also knew what he knew, murder is most certainly at least a possibility. There was a clear motive, a possible method, and a plausibly deniable story already prepared and ready for the taking. Someone just had to make it happen.

Interestingly, in researching his life, I discovered yet another piece of the puzzle that might get us closer to determining what happened. In late 1959, ABL was visiting family in Miami on a stop-over on his way to Cuba, a trip I had never heard about or seen a reference to in any of his remaining papers. He visited Montego Bay, Jamaica, from June 22–July 7, 1959, on an earlier trip to the Caribbean. Later, with Fidel Castro, Che Guevara, and other revolutionaries in power in Havana, the Mafia and US corporations were ousted from the island nation, which was still very much in revolutionary fervor mode; ABL went on his way to Cuba "chasing some guy," according to family members. At the same time, in a remarkable twist, both the Mafia *and* the CIA worked together against Cuba. All the while, Bobby Kennedy loudly proclaimed a war on organized crime.

I wonder this unappetizing thought: Is it possible that someone sent ABL to Cuba to assassinate Castro? Why in the world was he traveling *to* Cuba when all other Americans had left or were forced to leave? On the surface of it, who better than a highly trained G-Man/spy/investigator/bug planter/surveillance expert to go to Cuba at the request of—who? Could the Mob have pressured him to go— knowing that in his investigations with Marilyn that he had found out too much? An exchange could have played itself out like this:

"We will let you off the hook if you do something for us."

"Do something?" ABL asked.

"Yes," the mobster replied. "Go down to Havana and assassinate that bastard Castro."

"And if I don't?"

"You don't want to know that answer. We know where you live."

Could this explain why he was so scared while visiting family in Florida right before leaving? Could this be the real reason he went to Cuba? It is not widely known, but the US, in various guises, attempted to assassinate Castro more than six hundred times, including eighty attempts after the revolution and before ABL's death. Could one of those potentially involved have been ABL, an ardent right-winger? From 1959 until August 1962, during both the Eisenhower presidency (whom ABL loved) and the Kennedy Administration (whom ABL loathed), there were attempts to illegally kill a leader of another sovereign country involving everyone from the Mafia to one of Castro's ex-girlfriends and maybe even ABL. One ploy devised by the CIA involved contaminating a wetsuit with tuberculosis bacteria and a Madura fungus intended to cause a destructive skin ailment, then gifting it to Fidel via a third party.

Another one of the more well-known plots involved the CIA dispatching an employee of Howard Hughes (who ABL had ferreted out of hiding *twice*) named Robert Maheu. Maheu recruited well-known Mafia figures Roselli, Giancana, and Santo Trafficante to poison Castro's food with botulinum toxin, which would have killed him almost instantly. The plot failed after Castro stopped going to the restaurant where they planned to serve the infected food.[65]

All these mobsters were involved in Marilyn Monroe's world, with which ABL was entwined. There is every possibility that ABL would have known them and they would have known him. Who better than an ex-FBI agent turned private eye to the stars and who had become increasingly addicted to alcohol to recruit to do the dirty work, especially if they had dirt on him such as his possible sexual orientation?

We will probably never know who ABL chased after in Cuba, but according to his nephew when I interviewed him several years ago, he was a "nervous wreck, entirely stressed out like I have never seen a person before," unable to sleep, and deeply uneasy about his trip. Everything we know about US antagonism toward Cuba since the revolution in 1958, including the failed Bay of Pigs invasion and subsequent animosity toward the Kennedy administration from those involved—who felt betrayed by the lack of promised air cover—adds another layer of mystery to ABL's already enigmatic life. Could the

---

[65]"When Uncle Sam Desperately Wanted to Whack Fidel" in *Jacobin* (Issue 49, Spring 2023), p. 94.

guy chased have been connected?

Alas, none of this was ever properly investigated, and his death certificate reflects the story that my grandfather simply died from natural causes. Some family members held his first funeral at Pierce Brothers Chapel in Beverly Hills. Then his body went back to Alabama in a bolted shut casket, necessitating an unusual and very rare, closed coffin, second funeral, and burial, causing great consternation amongst the family, all of whom wondered why it was impossible to open the box in which ABL would lay forever. Was someone, somewhere, trying to hide something?

Larry Godbold, who attended the funeral, remembered it this way: "My parents were discussing the casket when he got flown out here, and it was a closed casket, and they had to tell Grandma that it was alright that it was a closed casket. I remember them saying: 'Well, we'll tell her that during shipping, he got bruised up or something.' There was some reason they didn't want the casket to be easily opened, which was unusual in our family. They couldn't open the casket."

Finally, they buried him in Magnolia Cemetery under a simple flat gravestone with only his name mentioned, where it all began, back in Greenville, Alabama, where he lies to this day, the many adventures of his life largely unknown to the public at large.

Chapter 13

A Life in the Deep Closet?

In his 1993 book *The Secret Life of J. Edgar Hoover*, author Anthony Summers claims that despite Hoover's vicious public stances against homosexuality and his obsession with including sexual indiscretions within secret files, Hoover himself was closeted (secretly gay). Summers alleges that his deputy Clyde Tolson was his private partner for many years. Summers wrote, "Clyde Tolson joined the FBI in 1928 and rose to become assistant director within three years. He and Edgar became lovers and vacationed together every year. Each liked to photograph each other ..."[66]

The book further asserts that Hoover possibly faced extortion due to his sexual orientation: "... top organized crime figures Meyer Lansky and Frank Costello obtained photos of Hoover's alleged homosexual activity with long-time aide Clyde Tolson and used them to ensure that the FBI did not target their illegal activities."[67]

In an effort to dissuade anyone from suspecting that political

---

[66]Anthony Summers, *The Secret Life of J. Edgar Hoover*, Pocket Books, 1993, Photo caption mid-book, photos 10-12.

[67]https://www.latimes.com/archives/la-xpm-1993-02-06-mn-1078-story.html.

leaders at the time had any inkling of an inclination toward loving members of their sex, specific and common measures were often undertaken by gay men. They sought to project stereotypes deemed as the opposite by society at large. And yet, these often contradicted each other. There was an expectation that men would marry, have a child, buy a home, engage in sports, attend the horse races, and otherwise project masculinity. Gay men would do the same, nipping any rumors of gayness in the bud ASAP.

At the same time, however, Hoover would prefer to do some things that could easily create suspicions. As Elias noted, "Hoover preferred to hire single men, arguing that they were less encumbered by familial obligations and could privilege the job above all else."[68] In what Elias has described as a sense of "surveillance state masculinity," society forced men to do nothing that would provoke unwanted questions due to prevailing sentiments. He added, "… Any man who did not actively affirm and reaffirm his masculinity and accompanying heterosexuality was open to constant suspicion."[69] He continued, "Both Hoover and McCarthy conspicuously performed his masculinity, even while being hounded by rumors and insinuations that he was 'queer' or a 'sissy,' and thus insufficiently manly to guard the country's moral well-being and ensure its security."[70] But despite these measures, suspicions remained.

Some of Hoover's closest allies attempted to refute these allegations, and none more so than a former FBI agent named Cartha DeLoach.[71] In a blatantly pro-Hoover book, DeLoach clumsily and archaically attempts to refute the numerous allegations of Hoover's hidden sexual orientation, including his lifelong relationship with Tolson. Using rather questionable and outdated criteria of same-sex orientation, DeLoach unconvincingly wrote that "… neither Hoover nor Tolson was the least bit effeminate. Both were tough and manly. Hoover was a bulldog. Tolson was a strapping, healthy fellow in his

---

[68]Christopher M. Elias, *Gossip Men: J. Edgar Hoover, Joe McCarthy, Roy Cohn, and the Politics of Insinuation*, University of Chicago Press, 2021, p. 54
[69]Id, p. 43.
[70]Id, p. 5.
[71]Supra, DeLoach.

youth. He played first base on the FBI's champion baseball team, and there wasn't the slightest sign of weakness or 'prettiness' in his face. He was certainly more of a man than Mr. Summers, and I've seen both at close quarters."[72]

After my dad finally started telling me stories about his father, I remember asking him outright on the eighteenth fairway of a beautiful golf course in Palm Desert, California, having built up the courage to do so over the previous seventeen holes, if he thought it might be possible that his father might have also been gay. My dad quickly dismissed what to him was an outlandish question from his pro-gay rights son. ABL, the consummate networker, always wrote letters to everyone he knew and seemed to know just about everyone wherever he lived, even those who dabbled in what at the time was very much the hidden, even forbidden, arts surely leave us wondering.

In a clue against his possible homosexuality, one first-hand witness, my mother, told me, "We went to his apartment one night for dinner, and there was a knock on the door. It was a female hooker. "Go away, go away, come back another night," he whispered to the unwanted visitor. This event may have occurred precisely as my mother recalled it. But what if the "female hooker" was a 1960s Hollywood transvestite or early transsexual, something not all that uncommon then or now? What if—in yet another effort to hide his sexuality—ABL took the utmost care and only interacted with sex workers who were men dressed as women? I don't know. I wasn't there. But this surely seems possible.

I have no direct proof that ABL was or was not a member of the gay community, at least at times. Yet, quite a few circumstantial clues —when put together in a row—reveal that things could have possibly evolved in this direction. Having accessed the personal letters between ABL and Hoover, I noted that many of these letters convey a sense of closeness and familiarity, contrasting sharply with the reprimands and serious tones found in their other correspondence. In fact, it feels very much like the closeness of ABL and Hoover could have been more than sufficient to have been the real reason for his dismissal—driven

---

[72]Id., p. 63.

by Hoover's deputy and lover, a deeply jealous Clyde Tolson. Beyond the letters, in early April 1938, ABL received a blurry, soft-focused type of photograph from Hoover on which he wrote, "To A.B. Leckie, with cordial regards from your friend, J. Edgar Hoover 4/2/38." Again, this may be perfectly innocent, but there is an incongruity to it that is hard to define or reconcile.

What does this gift mean? Was it simply a kind gesture, or was it intended to convey more than that, a subtle hint of an invitation for more? Why did he gift him this photo at precisely the same time officials reprimanded ABL? What was it, Hoover? Friend or foe? Another 1938 letter from Hoover thanked ABL for a happy birthday telegram and New Year's greetings. He wrote, "… I want you to know how deeply appreciative I am of you for remembering me." This could have meant absolutely nothing more than a friendly exchange, but perhaps Hoover's deputy might have become nervous about this seemingly ever-closer embrace. Could the real reason Hoover eventually pushed ABL out of the agency have had an amorous edge? In their totality, they make me wonder just how close these men were to one another. Was it perhaps more than just a working relationship or the early stages of something else that may have lasted for decades after his painful departure from the FBI? Was love in the air in the late 1930s in Washington DC?

Hoover's closeness with a series of other men is legendary and increasingly well-known. Of course, first and foremost was Clyde Tolson, his deputy, his confidant, and his lover. As leading Hoover historian Beverly Gage opines: "If he was married to anyone, it was to Clyde Tolson, his famously loyal associate director … Where Hoover went, Tolson went too: not only to the office but to the nightclub and the racetrack, on vacations and out for weeknight dinners, to family events and White House receptions. They were, in essence, a couple, though almost nobody—especially Hoover—referred to them that way."[73] She continued, "While we have no detailed record of what transpired behind closed doors, it seems safe to say that Hoover was

---

[73]Supra, Gage, p. xii.

not having sex with women."[74]

But Hoover was enamoured with many other men besides Tolson. Guy Hottel, an agent with special access to and treatment by Hoover, also bore many of the same hallmarks of ABL's quick rise through the ranks at the FBI. Hottel tried to dismiss any suggestion that he received favorable treatment and said, "You got quick promotion in those days."[75] Others have suggested a more complicated narrative: that Hoover went out of his way for Hottel to protect his own secrets. In later years, Hottel allegedly boasted that he had seen Hoover and Tolson involved in "sex parties" at Hoover's house, you know, "with the boys"—indeed, that Hoover coerced his Bureau subordinates into attending these gatherings as a rite of passage."[76]

According to Gage, "The most that can be said is that the stories fit with Hoover's pattern of using his status as FBI director to develop intimate relationships with his subordinates. His right to do so was baked into Bureau culture: homosocial intensity, strict hierarchy, and the need for employees always to please and placate the boss. At the very least, Hottel's status as a close friend and social favorite helps to explain his own peculiar record. In 1936 alone, he earned reprimands for offending the Colombian ambassador, playing golf while on call, and failing to restrain drunken companions at the Congressional Country Club. The following year, Hoover appointed him special agent in charge of the Washington field office."[77] Gage noted, "Of more immediate consequence for Tolson was the impending marriage of Guy Hottel. Tolson and Hottel had lived together off and on since college, fraternity brothers playing out an extended adolescence. Hottel's departure left Tolson, like Hoover, more alone than he had been in years, the routine commitments of his life thrown into flux."[78] ABL's experiences mirrored these so closely that changing the names in this history would still result in an accurate story.

---

[74]Id, p. 137.

[75]Id, p. 184.

[76]Id, p. 184.

[77]Id, p. 184.

[78]Id, p. 221.

Concerning Hoover's best friend at Kappa Alpha, Thomas Frank Baughman, Gage wrote, "Hoover's closeness with Baughman raises a question that would persist throughout his adult life: was this just a friendship?

Or was it a romantic, even sexual, relationship? Same-sex relationships were not unheard of at GW, where interested students occasionally staged clandestine dances and social events in out-of-the-way spots. Indeed, fraternities themselves became places of quiet same-sex experimentation."[79]

But by far, the most widely discussed "special friend" of Hoover was Melvin Purvis. Just like with ABL, Hoover and Purvis wrote countless personal letters to one another, many of which were highly private, addressing sexual and other matters. Like ABL, Purvis came from the South. As if describing the Hoover and ABL letters, Gage used the following language to outline the nature of the correspondence between Purvis and Hoover. She said, "Their banter is elusive, the precise nature of their mutual interest in such matters obscured beneath layers of propriety and evasive code."[80]

In the early years, Hoover would ask Purvis to carry out secret activities. In the process, Purvis worked his way up, becoming one of the most famous FBI agents of all time. The two men grew incredibly close. Gage continued, "Other Bureau executives continued to question Purvis's temperament and leadership abilities. 'He is a little impatient for things to happen,' Clegg noted in 1932, even as he praised Purvis's 'loyalty.' Hoover, though, had already made up his mind to give Purvis the biggest reward yet. In October 1932, he appointed Purvis special agent in charge at Chicago, one of the Bureau's largest and most important field offices."[81] ABL, of course, took on that very same job just a few short years later.

Unfortunately for Purvis, whatever love Hoover may have felt for him, Purvis' rise induced feelings of jealousy more than anything else, and by the end of 1935, Purvis lost his position. Again, a remarkable

---

[79]Id, p. 47.

[80]Id, p. 142.

[81]Id, p. 146.

series of events incredibly similar to the fate suffered by ABL.

Hoover's notable treatment of Tolson, Purvis, Hottel, and Baumann and his subsequent abuse of ABL highlights striking similarities. Their common traits raise the likelihood of more than a friendship between ABL and his boss, as had been the case with Purvis. It was never written down, and no films of romance exist, but reading between an ever-growing number of lines, it seems clear that there was something more in both cases.

In language that could have described ABL almost verbatim, as much as it did in describing Purvis' fall from Hoover's grace, "Purvis was now his rival rather than his subordinate. In November [1934], an inspection team noted that Purvis was flouting Hoover's rules, sauntering in late, allowing stenographers to smoke on the premises, and treating the office as a personal hangout, with 'dirty underwear and shirts' scattered throughout. '[Purvis] is extremely temperamental, egotistical,' Hoover's inspection team warned, 'He had been giving more and more time to his own personal interests and to his social activities than he had been giving to the office which he represents.' In March 1935, rumors around Chicago said Purvis had been spotted drunk at a party, brandishing a gun and shouting incoherently."[82]

Mirroring his treatment of ABL, "Hoover undertook a campaign of harassment so petty and vindictive that it can be explained only in personal terms. He transferred Purvis to Charlotte, North Carolina, stripping him of his authority at the famed Chicago office. Along the way, he began to second-guess nearly everything Purvis did. When Purvis authorized the use of a Bureau car to deliver a fugitive to Alcatraz, for instance, Hoover sent an indignant memo about the proper use of official vehicles ... Though the public still knew him as Hoover's G-Man par excellence, he resigned from the Bureau in early July 1935, explaining to the press that his decision was 'purely personal.'"[83]

It is extraordinary how similarly Hoover treated ABL just a few years later. Indeed, in reference to his new best friend, Tolson, Gage

---

[82]Id, p. 180.
[83]Id.

noted that, "Some of Tolson's disdain for Purvis may have stemmed from personal or professional jealousy."[84] She added that, "Columns expressing doubt about Hoover's dating record implied that Tolson was a 'woman hater' and 'woman-dodger' who had deliberately chosen life with his charismatic male boss. Melvin Purvis—still the country's most famous G-Man, aside from Hoover—provided a convenient point of contrast. Rumors in the spring of 1938 suggested that he planned to marry his childhood sweetheart."

Hoover's homosexuality is increasingly well-known and accepted. But he was not alone within the law enforcement world in this regard in mid-20th-century America. Joseph McCarthy, with whom ABL also worked, as well as Roy Cohn, a leading lawyer at the HUAC, were also rumored to have been gay. The August 1954 cover of the magazine *Celebrity* advertised a story entitled "The Men in McCarthy's Life," insinuating his potential interest in the same sex. Although McCarthy eventually married his longtime secretary, Jean Kerr (reminiscent of ABL marrying Della), "... rumors were circulating that Cohn and McCarthy—and Hoover—has some of the same 'perverted' sexual proclivities they denounced in their opponents. There were even whispers that McCarthy's recent wedding was an attempt to silence that talk. And although McCarthy's cult of personality had helped Republicans win major gains in 1952, members of the Eisenhower administration were entertaining the possibility that the rumors about him and his staffers were not so far-fetched after all."[85] He continued, "Stories claiming that McCarthy was a homosexual had circulated seemingly since the moment he entered the national spotlight in early 1950."[86]

And yet, as was typical at the time, the more one sought to hide their own sexuality, the more viciously one sought to "out" others less powerful than themselves. Tye noted that, "Communists were Joe McCarthy's favorite bogeyman but not his only ones. Homosexuals were another focus, one fraught with opportunity as well as peril for

---

[84]Id, p. 182.

[85]Supra, Elias, pp. 162-163.

[86]Id, 173-174.

the bachelor senator. And much as he was playing an essential role in perpetuating the Red Scare, he also utilized his trademark tactics and strategies to ignite and sustain what became known as the Lavender Scare. The threat, as McCarthy shouted it, was that homosexuals working for agencies like the State Department were living closeted lives, petrified they might be exposed and were, therefore, prime targets for blackmail by Soviet spymasters."[87] Tye again asked, "Was the gay-bashing senator himself gay? The gossip was constant and lurid, with tales of him having affairs with one man in Wausau and another in Milwaukee and becoming entangled with young bellboys and elevator operators. And it wasn't just what he did but whom he affiliated with … Thankfully for Joe, the judge who mattered most, Hoover, applied more forgiving standards. The FBI boss kept his pledge to stay quiet, which saved his friend McCarthy, while giving Hoover the leverage he sought over every politician in Washington."[88]

Who really ever knows the deep inner workings of other people, including family members, unless they share their secrets (or if confirming written or film evidence exists)? I have no conclusive information that points undisputedly to ABL's sexual proclivities. I personally have no problem whatsoever with homosexuality nor bisexuality, or even asexuality; whatever a person wishes to do or not to do in the bedroom is fine with me and always has been, as long as everyone in the same bedroom is a willing participant and above the age of consent. If anything, I would be overjoyed if ABL had explored gay love, being courageous enough to listen to his sexual urges and act on them. During his time in history, homosexuality was not only illegal in many jurisdictions but a career killer—and a tag that would

---

[87]Supra, Tye, p. 163. The footnote reads: "Ironically, the most compelling instance of that vulnerability to blackmail occurred when J. Edgar Hoover successfully threatened to unmask various homosexual bureaucrats unless they become his informants." (cites: Dean, Imperial Brotherhood, 166) —Tye. See also: "No hindrance to a man's masculinity was greater than homosexuality, which was generally viewed as incompatible with the attributes that made men moral, Christian, and decent. It deeply troubled Americans during the interwar years that signs of homosexuality seemed to be everywhere." (p. 115), Supra, Elias.
[88]Id, Tye, p. 166.

label people forevermore.

This was especially so during the time of ABL's working life. As is well known, people who actively pursued a gay way of life, both male and female, went to extraordinary lengths to hide it. Anyone who was even suspected of being gay, whether through rumor, innuendo, gossip, or, in some rare instances, actual evidence, would face a lifelong battle to repair their reputation. That one's sexuality—something which people are now accepted to have been born with—could be used in this way seems shocking today in an era where a growing majority of countries fully accept gay marriage and legally prohibit discrimination against people on the grounds of their sexuality. But during the 1930s and beyond, being gay in the US was the equivalent of having the "scarlet letter" tattooed onto one's shirt.

ABL married twice, once to my grandmother and then to Hoover's former secretary, Della. He fathered one child: my father. He moved in with a man in his mid-50s and stayed with him in an apartment until the time of his death. He hung out in known gay locales such as Venice Beach, San Francisco, and elsewhere. He spent his days and nights at a bar called the Tail o' the Cock and hobnobbed with many of Hollywood's elite, many known to be gay. Two of his highest-profile jobs—with the FBI and the HUAC—saw him hired by two extremely powerful gentlemen—Hoover and McCarthy—who were themselves, both during and after their lives, strongly suspected of being closeted. If one was seeking to hide one's sexuality, would they not be far more likely to hire someone in the very same position than someone else who might expose them?

No one will probably ever know if ABL was straight, gay, bisexual, or anything else. There is evidence and indication in both directions. But if we seek a reason for his severe alcoholism in his later years, the need to conceal his true self from the world and the constant fear of public labelling as "gay" would surely suffice to drive someone to drink. Maybe it was simply built, and he was destined to become a drunk. Maybe it was his unceremonious departure from the FBI. Or maybe it was the secret that he took to the grave.

Interestingly, although my father destroyed almost all of my grandad's papers, he managed to set aside and keep a series of letters he received following his father's parting, and more than a few of them reference secrets or hidden aspects of ABL's life. One of these noted, "I am so glad that you were inclined to give me a little more detail concerning my good friend. I had no idea that our exchange of correspondence would go into his files. There was, indeed, a real quality of friendship between us …"

If there is any indication of just what could have been in those countless thousands of pages of files, in a condolence letter that did survive, one of ABL's friends wrote the following to my father: "I trust there are not too many indiscretions in any letters of mine he may have kept, since he and I were completely honest friends and shared the good and the bad quite wholeheartedly. Two mutual events in our lives will always stand out in my memory, but a letter is no place to describe them, and I know he will understand if I grin every time I think of them." Oh, how I wish I knew what those two events were; I am certain they are two of many thousands in the extraordinary life he lived.

It is certainly possible that Hoover's and his deputy's nerves were frayed somewhat during what became ABL's final months in the Bureau. Just two days after receiving that famous photo, Hoover wrote tersely to ABL, declining what might have been a quid pro quo of free baseball game tickets for the season opener—a desperate attempt, perhaps, to spend quality time in public with a man who had become more than just a boss. He received another letter from Tolson some days after that and then another from Hoover admonishing him for working too many hours of overtime a day, with orders to work less. Not long after that, he was gone for good.

One of the most curious letters from Hoover dates from May 26, 1955, more than a decade and a half after leaving the FBI, where he said in what surely could be an intentional double *entendre*, "I recall very well indeed the waitress at the Ambassador Hotel Coffee Shop whom you mentioned. It is always a pleasure for me to see her when I am in Los Angeles, and I was glad to know that you had met and talked with her. Sincerely, JEH." Hoover first forced ABL out of his beloved FBI in 1939, and then a full sixteen years later, he wrote that. Something very fishy sure seems to be going on here.

Chapter 14

Coming Full Circle

One of the saddest aspects of the life of my grandfather happened after his death. As outlined in Chapter 10, for whatever reason, late in his life, he decided to marry Della Sayre, his second wife. From pictures of the wedding, it appears superficially that he was happy as could be on the day of the nuptials—in an era well before pre-nuptial agreements became all the rage, particularly in LA and Hollywood. Though he circulated among the political and social elites of the day, ABL was upper middle class at the time of his death.

The expectation, of course, was that my father, as the only child, would inherit the bulk of his father's estate. His will precisely envisages that. However, as noted above, almost immediately after his death, Della made claims against his estate, claiming that ABL had promised her fifty thousand dollars but never paid it. Della filed lawsuits and created a range of obstacles to closing the estate. This battle went on for years. In October 1965, my father noted in a telegram to ABL's brother Dulin that, "Della is still causing trouble, but I hope we are approaching the end of her efforts in preventing the distribution of the estate."

I never even knew of Della's existence until I began researching the life story of my grandfather, so I have no first-hand experience in knowing her. Interviewing people who knew her and reviewing a wide range of documents about her, including countless direct quotes taken under oath during depositions, it is abundantly clear that she was extremely angry at ABL for ending their marriage. She was even more perturbed that ABL never provided her with the financial resources she seemed to expect, either in life or after his death. Reading through more than one hundred pages of her sworn testimony provides insight into her frame of mind following his death as I seek to understand the very nature of their unusual and short-lived marriage.

One of the documents unearthed contains a list of expenses made by ABL during his marriage some thirteen months prior to his death. One of these entries involves an expenditure of $10.01 for American Airlines: "This is the night I left for Jamaica on business. I gave Della one hundred dollars in cash when I left her in San Diego that same evening. This $10.01 was an additional plane on another airline."

Another document, an inheritance tax affidavit, rather interestingly lists his debts at the time of his death, which amounted to less than 10% of his assets. These include several restaurant bills from places including Cave de Roys, Hoefly's, Kelly's, the Ambassador, and, of course, the Tail o' the Cock for an outstanding balance of $13.67. Presumably, these were among the last places ABL ever dined, showing again that he spent much of his time wining and dining the LA nights away.

At a hearing as part of the divorce trial on February 11, 1962, Della claimed that ABL had evicted her and that he had treated her with extreme cruelty, leading her to have a heart attack. The exchanges between Della and the attorneys on the stand are instructive. Her lawyer asked her, "Would you state briefly, and in your own words, in what manner Mr. Leckie treated you with extreme cruelty?"

She replied, "He was—he drank excessively and constantly. I had to do his secretarial work for him. I was not only a wife. I was a secretary. He treated me as a convenience. He spent most of his time at the Tail o' the Cock, drinking and socializing. He would buy a fifth of bourbon every night and consume it at home. He drank when I was ill in bed in his apartment with paralysis of the neck. He refused me medical attention."

The Court then asked, "And he finally evicted you?"

She replied, "I was in San Diego and suffered a heart attack."

"And how did this course of conduct affect you? You got a heart attack, is that right?" asked the Court.

Della replied, "I had a heart attack. The doctor diagnosed it as being precipitated by severe emotional distress."

Another ABL mystery concerns a woman, Marie Dickinson, who I had also never heard of prior to exploring his life. In a small file containing names and addresses written in the handwriting of my father and labeled as "Est. of Leckie," we find an entry for Marie Dickinson with two addresses in Los Alamitos, a suburb of LA made famous by its well-known horse racing track, a place frequented by my father and his father.

Having been extremely unenthusiastically brought along to "the track" by my well-intentioned father on numerous occasions during my younger years, I have a strong aversion to horseracing, gambling, and everything associated with this particular vice. On my father's final visit to my current home in Australia just a year before his death in 2016, instead of wanting to see our countless pristine beaches, forests, wineries, incredible food offerings, or other things on offer, he only wanted to go to the races. As much as I wanted him to be happy and enjoy his company, after a long fourteen-hour flight from LA, I agreed to take him to the horse races twice, once to the famous Flemington Racetrack and the other at the track in Mornington. We first went to Flemington, a suburb of the great city of Melbourne, which required parking far from the entrance. The three of us, my father, my father-in-law, Wesley, and I ambled from the dirt parking area to the massive track famous for the appalling drunkenness of its patrons on one of the worst days of the year. Known as the Melbourne Cup, people dress up in a horrendous display of extreme tawdriness— men in their tuxes and other hideous garments and the women unstable on their feet because of their absurd heels and wearing hats of the gaudiest sort. I have never been there on that particular day and most certainly never will—thank goodness—but the news blasts it every year. It even serves as a public holiday in the state of Victoria, yet another sign of Australia's incredible weakness in resisting the pull to gamble. Australia surely has much to offer, but its propensity to wager on everything, anytime, any day, is surely one of my least favorite things about my latest territorial abode. In Australia, one can even bet during AFL football games mid-match, not just on who will win or lose but who will score next, how long the goal kick would be, who would get the assist, which end of the stadium the goal would be scored in, and everything else. Gambling ads are all over both TV and radio, and awful places called TABs are found everywhere—so people can part with their money just a little more easily.

That day at Flemington, as much as my dear old dad enjoyed it, was disdained by me at a far higher level. "Look at their grandeur, tiger. Such beautiful animals. Incredible," he would say as he decided on which horse to bet in the next race. He loved the races, and I loved seeing him enjoy them so much, but I just couldn't share in it. After waiting in a long line to bet on the next race, surrounded by so many sad characters thinking they were finally going to strike it rich, virtually all of whom depressingly had a beer or other drink in hand, universally reeking that horrible odor of people who have had one too many, I just had to get out of there.

Having travelled as much as I have across the world countless times, including to hundreds of slums, war zones, disaster settings, and other less-than-easy places, my tolerance level for difficult and crowded places is reasonably high. However, at the track, all tolerance just drains out of me, and any hope I have for humanity fades into an opaque and bleak vision that, in fact, we are all doomed. Thankfully, I brought work with me in the car, and after twenty minutes inside that hell zone, I got the keys from Wesley and left them to enjoy the rest of the day. I spent the next six hours in and around the car working on a funding proposal, which luckily for me, was funded a few months later, turning me and my NGO over for the next year.

A few days later, back at home on the quiet peninsula where we live, my dad couldn't think of anything else he wanted to do. He asked if we could go to the races again. He was eighty-two years old then, and whatever inquisitiveness he had throughout life, which was indeed quite considerable, had sort of drained out of him, leaving just the races as something big to anticipate. Luckily, in the small town of Mornington there happened to be races on, so we took him and my mother to the track and dropped them at the entrance. I couldn't bear another day of horses facing the whips, drunk gamblers misbehaving, and the whole depressing scene. Hours later, we picked them up, and they'd had a great time. They met a local couple who they spent the day with, watching the *gigis* (horses), and were positively bubbly when we picked them up.

I partly believe my father liked the races so much, an unconscious thing to a man who rarely to never spoke of his emotions, because races reminded him of his dad. ABL's interest in the track was at least as large as his son's and must have been driven partly by his tendency during his early years to emulate Hoover's pastimes. Hoover and his boyfriend Tolson frequently visited the races, in particular to Del Mar in between LA and San Diego during their annual jaunts to La Jolla, where I spent many a Sunday with my dad trying to get excited. It only left me with a lifelong dislike of everything linked to those sad locales, wherever they are. Horses, gamblers, and drunks are not my scene.

What sets the mystery woman Marie Dickinson apart from the other names on the list is a series of notes, also in my father's handwriting, written on different dates in different colors of pen ink, outlining a series of intriguing details. The first note lists her name and then proceeds—unlike anyone else on the list of names and addresses —her driving license number, her social security number, and her Chevrolet license plate number. It lists her mother-in-law, who was a resident at the time in Modesto. These entries appear in black ink.

Then a second entry written in blue ink notes, "Marie Dickinson leads" and then lists a few names and phone numbers that someone, likely my father as the executor of the estate, called in his quest to find her. But who was she? Why have I only uncovered her existence now? The strangest entry appears on the same side of the same page but in green ink. The first line notes, "Marie H. Dickinson 10-15-65 to 8-15-66 $136.25 per mo." It then lists the same data as before, such as her driving license. Then, the final entry, probably written during the fourth time he added to the list, this time again in black ink, my father wrote, "Marie met AB March 17, 1962—saw Marie here prior. I saw Marie a couple of times during the week. Couple of weeks that she wouldn't see her—he was sick—told Carlos won liquor—colorful. (2/12—card received)—She had taken him (still) May–August (John Cleary—bartender). It continues on the reverse side of the page with the following: "1—Raining first ride to work, 2—state of mind—a) told her where and what, b) three mornings a week gave ride to work —c) not out to dinner because of diabetes, d) went to dinner with Carlos; 3—Della was furious on wash-cloth—rain clothes; 4. (2-1-62 —went to dinner with him, 2-23-62 went to dinner with him); 5. 2-1-62; 6. NO LOVE IN FIRST PLACE—2-1-62—(A) Great relief; (B) Said going with her steady. Marie would drive up here often—or he would see."

What am I to make of this? When one combines the phrases "going steady," regular payments, and the anger of ABL's second wife, one may be able to conclude that ole ABL might have had something going on in private—that only now sees the light of day. This may be conclusive proof that he was not entirely gay, but at the same time, it may also provide another reason why my father was so reluctant to speak about his father, as he only uncovered this side of his dad after his death. His way of dealing with it was to pretend to the world that it never happened. I can't help thinking how Della might have reacted to this news.

With such much mystery surrounding both ABL's life and the death, holding the original of his death certificate in my hand for the first time felt incredibly powerful. Knowing what we know now about his final days, the unpretentious and seemingly convincing cause of death—diabetes mellitus—seems almost too simple to be true. That he died at the age of only fifty-seven, and I almost died, too, at precisely the same age. That holds some significance, at least to me. I know for certain that my illness so easily could have removed me from life. Had it not been for an unfathomable will to live and do more, I am certain I would have died. Despite all of the never-ending pain and anguish I endured for eight solid months, staring down the Grim Reaper every waking moment for month after month and almost being born anew after the worst of the illness had passed, by pure will and the assistance of extraordinary doctors, I survived. In the three years since then, I have never physically felt better, never been more productive, having written nine full-length books during that time, and have never been more grateful for life. I had and still have everything to live for, and I can't help thinking that had ABL had a reason to live, he would have chosen that path.

Chapter I5

At Last, I Know You Grandad, You Rascal

It took me six decades to begin to get to know my dad's dad, who died sixty-three years ago in August 1962, just like Marilyn. I've discovered some similarities, tried to understand our many differences, especially our worldviews, and in the process, uncovered a few clues about his remarkable life. At a certain moment, I picked up a particularly clear and well-focused photograph from the 1930s and peered deeply into his eyes, looking, searching, trying to feel his essence. After a few moments, I then spoke with my granddad for the very first time:

> *I know you so much better now, Grandad, you little rascal, you. I see now at least some of the things we shared but also where we diverged, sometimes rather dramatically. We both fled the towns of our upbringing just as soon as we could after high school, and we both played golf and ran track. We both had a lot to do with the UN and even both wrote about the importance of a safe home for people everywhere. We both have had an incredible drive and forms of ambition that led us far from home. You stuck to America, and I chose the world.*

You had the Tail o' the Cock as your hangout spot; I had airplanes, concerts, and the world's human rights hot spots as my go-to places, and I still do. You had a boss who both raised you up and cut you down, and luckily for me, I've been able to be my own boss throughout my career. You drank a lot; I used to drink a little, but never like you, and was surely never addicted to that particular vice, though there may have been others. You died when you were just fifty-seven, and in another near coincidence, I came within inches of doing the same, suddenly and without warning being struck down by a brutal case of severe and acute gallstone-induced pancreatitis, which left me languishing in pain for sixty-five days in hospital where I underwent nine surgeries before things finally turned around. For some strange reason, around the time I turned fifty-seven, about eleven months before I was struck down, I took my beautiful friends Nathan and Amber out to lunch near my current home in Australia to discuss some work plans and talked about you and how you died at fifty-seven. I mentioned to my friends that I had also just turned fifty-seven. The table went quiet, and then we all burst out laughing nervously, not knowing then how very close you and I would come to dying at the very same age.

It's not enough, but I do feel like I know you now, at least a little. We lived our lives in very different ways and chose very different professional paths. I know so much more now, but what keeps gnawing away at me, Granddad is what it was that remained so painfully unresolved within you that led to your lifelong addiction to the bottle. What were you trying to drown out in all those bottles of Early Times, and what might it have taken to get you to put the bottles down forever? Was it Hoover's rebuke? Repressed urges? Something else? I see you now before me, wondering if you can muster the courage to tell all, but you refrain.

So, it is only during nights of particularly lucid dreaming when my subconscious turns my ears in just the right direction and listening very closely, I can hear a voice I've never heard but one I recognize immediately, and it's you, a part of me. You're feeling free, bubbly, and I watch your jowls wobbling, hear a still present soft Southern accent, slightly baritone, notice a smirk of recognition and acceptance emerging, catch a whiff of Early Times, spot that protuberant abdomen as you utter, in equal parts pride and supple ascendancy, in the magic of a shared moment: "You know my grandson, my only grandson, if there was no me, there would have been no you. In this life, we are forever entwined. And while you're wondering, yes, they did take me out for knowing what they didn't want me to know. It wouldn't be the first time, nor the last; life is so short; make it matter." With a sense of urgency, I then hastily ask, "Who? Who did it," and with that, the dream fades, and again, I awaken with just as many questions as answers.

And so, the mystery remains. We choose neither our families (nor our neighbors, for that matter), yet our links to them, and often our happiness, are universally undeniable. By any measure, putting together this story led me to feel so much closer to my granddad than ever before. At the same time, coming to terms with some of the life trails he took will surely take me some time, and I already know that I will never truly understand some things. I'm sure that were we able to have a chat or a meal together, it would have been gregarious, full of energy, and sometimes heated by serious disagreements about fundamental matters of principle and divergent wishes for the world. There can be no shaking the facts that ABL opposed immigration, that he was so close and beholden to Hoover and all that he stood for, that he carried out espionage on countless people and institutions, that he worked actively in support of the ruthless McCarthy trials, and so much more, behaving like a piece of a bigger puzzle game I do not want and have never wanted to have anything to do with, recalling that these tendencies continue to play unpleasant roles in so many corners of our modern world.

At the same time, I feel the deepest sense of compassion for ABL's suffering, manifested in his tragic departure from his dream job, his troubled relationships, and, above all, his drinking himself into a regular alcoholic haze to drown out his hero, Hoover, forcing him out of the FBI. Perhaps, too, he lived with a secret about his sexuality—that he thought could only be dealt with by bars and whisky bottles—which, in the end, may have killed him. Perhaps he did know too much about too many people and that was what absolutely killed him more sixty-three years ago. Maybe he just pushed it to the limit one too many times. We may never know.

What we do know now, however, is that this man freely latched himself onto some of the most unsavory Americans of the last century. That leaves a legacy with a degree of tarnish that no polish will ever be able to shine away. As Beverly Gage reminded us, as if we needed reminding, ABL's hero was anything but a nice guy: "In the decades since his [Hoover's] death, the abuses exposed by the Church Committee have continued to define his legacy; his name conjures up images of backroom scheming and abuse of power, of secrets and lies and the politics of fear. He has been depicted as a racist and a demagogue, a single-minded seeker of power, a small-minded and twisted man intolerant of even his own desires—all rightly so. During his lifetime, Hoover did as much as any individual in government to contain and cripple movements seeking racial and social justice, thusly limiting the forms of democracy and governance that might have been possible. His actions damaged the lives of thousands of people—liberals and journalists, civil rights workers and congressmen, Black Panthers, and communists. It is only fitting that his targets should have their say and that their experiences should help define his legacy."[89]

It seems ABL may have escaped the worst Southern traits by leaving that region, and his intentions were mostly sincere. Investigating in all its forms may yield important information, but just as easily—as he learned himself—it can come back and rebound with brutal consequences.

Learning so much about ABL's career and life choices, far from being swayed to turn in such directions myself, understanding the life of my granddad just strengthens my very different alternative vision of human rights for everyone, all of us integral parts of a unified humanity desiring to live in a world of kindness, tolerance, and love.

---

[89]Supra, Gage, p. 731.

And with each remaining day, I awaken from those lucid dreams, then prepare for another day of working for a better world, embracing those who ABL may well have investigated, pushing for changes he would have opposed, and seeing all of humanity not as nationalities born of the legal fiction we call the nation-state—but as a single human family with a shared destiny that only a world citizen can truly comprehend. ABL and I may be entwined in this life, the lives before, and those to come, and for that, I am grateful. But in our views of the world and how we seek or sought to change it, I fear divergence, and not overlap, will prevail forevermore. Every little tidbit of new information keeps me going, and as I progress in uncovering more and more of this mysterious man, I just want to know more.

Would ABL have investigated me, the consummate lefty—me, the democratic socialist, human rights advocating, Green politics pioneer? What would he have done if instructed to spy on his own grandson? Just how close did the US get, during those dreary days, to the in-family spying that became famous in many dictatorships over the years, where even children could expose their parents? Is it possible that the highest echelons of political power in the US put so much pressure onto ABL—and Marilyn Monroe, for that matter—that both of them died far earlier than they should have had circumstances been different?

As my efforts on this book were coming to a close, I made two final discoveries. I came across two small business card-sized photographs at the bottom of a file, which I think encapsulate features of the life of my mysterious grandfather as I went through the files I had scoured many times before. Both seem to be taken around the same time, perhaps maybe even on the same day, judging from the similarities of the bathing costume ABL donned that day, probably in the mid-1920s along the California coastline, most likely in or near his favorite beachside haunt, Venice Beach. In one, he appears in sexist, misogynist, perhaps even women-hater mode making a gesture in the shape of a vagina with his hands, thumbs touching thumbs pointed northwards and index fingers touching pointing southward. He had a smirk on his face that is almost ghoulish and sly, a part of him showing a devious knowledge of a woman's genitalia. But the other part is far more worrisome. It is the look of a creepy man no woman would want to be alone with. It is the look of a man who would happily join a club dedicated to women haters in the form of the gruesome Bachelor's Club. I don't know which of these sides dominated him, but both provide me with far more anxiety than comfort.

The other photograph, the same size, takes on a whole different feeling. It is the essence of camp: two men in one-piece bathing suits, arm in arm, seductively intimate, both proudly looking towards the camera as if "in the know." The man with ABL resembles a young Jack Kerouac, his one-piecer all black and my grandad's black and white horizontal stripes. The Kerouac character leans slightly backward with a satisfied look as if the coastal rocks against which they are leaning provided a convenient hiding place for two closeted USC students to engage in a daytime quickie while the others frolicked in the surf. They both have their guard down. They are relaxed, without a worry in the world. They got away with it. For that singular moment in time, they were happy, perhaps not yet realizing the depths they would both need to go to hide their shared love for other men.

Having gotten to know him so much more than ever before all these decades later, I wish I knew even more. I could have discovered mountains more than I did if I'd had access to the files he left behind, but alas, I do not. My father received countless phone calls upon ABL's death from reporters across the country literally begging him for file access. Instinctively knowing what was in these files—a system of information management probably taught to ABL by Hoover himself, the most famous Keeper of the Files in American history—my careful lawyer father quickly went through some of these files. He decided they were so sensitive in so many ways—so he destroyed forever hundreds of perfectly organized, immaculately kept files about many important Americans, Marilyn included. My father's cousin, Chuck, noted that, according to my dad, these files contained, "Good stories and bad stories, and enough bad ones that they could have brought him into grief," so off they went into the fire—gone for good.

I still don't know the precise contents of ABL's autopsy nor what secrets lay hidden within the unreleased FBI files. I'm sure that much remains to be discovered, but for the moment, I know him like never before. I understand him and many of his motivations, even if I find many of them nothing less than repugnant.

I share one-quarter of my genome with you, ABL. And while I thank you for it, I know more than most that it is not our genes, nor our families, religion, culture, part of the world we come from, or anything else that inevitably determines who we turn out to be and how we decide to live our all too finite lives. Those of us lucky enough to have had access to the highest levels of education and experience and those, with or without such degrees, who chose to embrace life, learn from it, and maximize everything that it can offer know that our lives are determined by a countless series of events, of books, of people, of films, of travel, of food, of relationships, of music, of intoxicants, of love and of hate, and of everything else.

For ABL, a certain vision of America, and to a lesser degree, the world, drove him. He was both a classic and almost predictable outcome of the historical time in which he lived. The era of G-Men kept the world safe from both fascism and communism. A time of Hollywood as Tinsel Town, the place where dreams could be manufactured into reality. All of this put together may have been what killed him in the end. While he escaped the oppression of the South and made the gutsy, albeit perhaps socially necessary, move to California, he leaned heavily to the right on the political spectrum. Repressing the facts that his hero Hoover fired him, all the while having to hide at least a part of his sexuality, severely drove him to the bottle. As with all of us, he was both a hero and a person with weaknesses and flaws: imperfect, driven by desire, and likely unable to find true peace and contentment.

For me, I took an entirely different path. I left home as he did at the young age of seventeen. But for me, the choice was to move not just states but to become an expatriate. Ever since leaving the country that ABL fought so hard to promote, I have seen the world as a whole as my home and the entire human race as my family. I have fought very hard in more than eighty countries for justice and human rights. In the process have discovered my true self as a tiny component in the larger game of life. As ABL did, I nudged and pushed for what I believed in. But I did not seek to expose people's secrets nor spy on people unknowingly but tried to improve the human rights prospects of people everywhere. Decades ago, my path began to diverge from the worldview of my grandfather, about whom I knew so little. It continues to diverge to this day and perhaps always will. Part of my conviction that this is true stems from the simple truth that all of us are the same. All of us are humans, first and foremost. This basic understanding is the basis of the path I have strode for decades—and one I will continue until my final day.

Acknowledgments

The author would like to thank the following wonderful people for reviewing and commenting on earlier versions of this work: Jaap Schut, Brian Gorlick, Viraaj Akuthota, Kirsten Young, Pablo Rueda, Craig Brown, and Sid Vadessari. The author would also like to thank Larry Godbold, Maryanne Leckie, and Chuck Leckie for kindly sharing their first-hand stories of the life and times of Arthur Bernard Leckie.

During the process of writing this and eight other books since June 2021, I met a whole range of extraordinary people who have become close friends, even if we have only ever met on Zoom calls. I am infinitely thankful to Ron Schulz for his assistance and insights into all the intricacies of the world of trade publishing. My immense thanks, as well, to Ebony Hood and Jen Z. Marshall for their excellent editing work.